Once and Again

Doors Are Made for Walking Through
Not Just Once . . . but Once and Again

SD Brewer

ARCHWAY
PUBLISHING

Archway Publishing books may be ordered through booksellers or by contacting:

Archway Publishing
1663 Liberty Drive
Bloomington, IN 47403
www.archwaypublishing.com
1 (888) 242-5904

Because of the dynamic nature of the Internet, any web addresses or links contained in this book may have changed since publication and may no longer be valid. The views expressed in this work are solely those of the author and do not necessarily reflect the views of the publisher, and the publisher hereby disclaims any responsibility for them.

Any people depicted in stock imagery provided by Getty Images are models, and such images are being used for illustrative purposes only. Certain stock imagery © Getty Images.

ISBN: 978-1-4808-6099-5 (sc)
ISBN: 978-1-4808-6101-5 (hc)
ISBN: 978-1-4808-6100-8 (e)

Library of Congress Control Number: 2018903934

Print information available on the last page.

Archway Publishing rev. date: 04/25/2018

Dedicated to the one who called me Babe
and made my life complete.

Introduction

❧

Once again, I am plagued by nightmares.

Standing at the wood line as the night settles in, I can hear a rush
of water in the background and glimpse its reflection through
the leaves as I gaze below. Everything about me looks normal,
yet my body is frozen, listening for a Voice in the distance. My
heart has fallen. I am completely consumed. Gripped in fear.
Then I hear it again, louder this time than before: "Gone."

Something is terribly wrong; this my soul knows full well. Yet
I can't move. I turn to the left and right, looking for help, for a
familiar face, anything that would prove the words wrong. But I
can't move, and in the weight of darkness, I remain locked in place,
unable even to bend my knee to plead and pray it away. No tears

come, although I can feel my heart being ripped asunder by things I cannot see. I stand alone—helpless—even as the weight of the unrevealed chokes the life from my frame and my mind confirms the whisper coming once again through the descending dusk: "The answer you request of Me is not one I can give. All is gone. You need to call someone." And a smothering darkness falls …

Nightmares. For fifty years they have plagued me, going as far back as I can remember. They are my villain. I am their victim. They come in power, leaving me vulnerable—fully aware of my inadequacies and that I am physically isolated. Alone. Undone. Always in the dead of night … in the dark.

I guess that's why I enjoyed spending so much time in the hills behind our home as a youth. When I was by myself in the light of day, my life was like a musical as I sang to the heavens and twirled beneath the same. It was a dream not a nightmare … something beautiful.

1

My name is Sherry. I am a first born with an A-type personality, stretching back for long as I can remember. My mother can confirm this, but when she says it, it will not sound like a positive. I was and am independent, a.k.a., strong willed. Now, according who you ask, that is a good thing, but Mom would probably call it stubborn, and then she'd say I was like my dad. Dad would say the same thing but blame it on my mom. Yin or yang, I'll say I am too much like the two of them to be anything but a "mess."

The reality is that even as a toddler I was dreaming and trying to set off on adventures. I was only two when I decided to go to the grocery store … alone. We had just moved from a trailer park to an apartment in Little Rock off of Broadway; this was not a quiet spot like our former neighborhood, with swing sets, slides, and the songs of birds above, but a place FULL of traffic and traffic noise and concrete. In all honesty, I remember only two things about this event: what initiated my journey and the attempt to bring it to fruition.

One. I remember being at the grocery store in the checkout line. Some things really *never* do change; just as it is today, when you wait in line to pay, the racks are filled with candy, gossip, and intrigue. While Mom may have been reading magazine covers I only saw the candy! And what kid doesn't want candy? So naturally, when Mom finally had the opportunity to step forward and unload the buggy, she did—including me. Then I did what all children do: I stepped back and grabbed both hands full of candy! Okay, so then Mom did what all moms do and said, "Put it back. You can get some *next time* we come." Then after "helping" me put it back, she grabbed me up, paid for and picked up our groceries, and hauled me back across the street and up the outdoor staircase to our apartment.

Too young to understand that what she *really* meant was NO, it wasn't long before I was pushing open the unlocked screen door and crawling backwards down the narrow and open wooden stairs to the sidewalk below. That's when I encountered a problem I couldn't overcome with a two-year-old mind. I was standing where Mom had been standing when she crossed the road to go the store. I could physically see the grocery store, but the cars just kept zipping by and wouldn't stop. *Hmmmm*, what was the problem? They stopped when I stood here with Mom? I stood waiting. (And I've NEVER been good at waiting.) Waiting … waiting, and then it happened! My travel plans were brought to a sudden halt as the weight of a firm hand settled on my shoulder and another plopped across my backside. Unceremoniously, I was swept up by my mom and whisked off upstairs crying—not because I was hurt but because I still had NO candy. My first adventure was a failure. And now, knowing I was a runner, Mom always made sure the doors were locked, and I became a "ward" under close supervision. LOL

Months later I gained a baby brother, Frankie. I was edging three at the time and completely frustrated by all the months of talking about getting a baby and then being told when he FINALLY showed up that I could not play with him. So, off I went, back to pretending and dreaming alone with babies I *could* tote around and play with.

By the time my mom and dad told us we were getting *another* baby, I was six and my brother had just turned four, and we had moved three more times. This time we settled in the country, way down a dirt road, where there were hills and woods and room to run, in a community (can you call it that when there is only one house every quarter to half mile??) anyway in the area between Crosby and Mount Pisgah, where my parents had grown up.

We were now in the perfect place to have great adventures! *No traffic!* Okay, we did have some traffic, but it was so rare that when we heard a car coming, we'd race to the window to see which of our four neighbors was going someplace. *And* I guess it wasn't quite perfect, as we didn't have indoor plumbing, just an upgraded two-seater outhouse. That did make it quite a bit less than perfect, especially for a young girl who had discovered she was a bit afraid of the dark and had a bad habit of drinking all day long.

On the positive side, we did have a spring-fed well on the back porch where we could draw water up via a long, skinny metal cylinder. Once up we would—okay, an adult would—release it into a bucket as they still thought I was too little. Then they'd let us scoop it out in a tin cup to drink! It was always sooooo cold! Old school awesome!!! (I feel kind of sorry for those of you too young to have gotten the opportunity to experience that. Ya'll just keep thinking that that $7 coffee is the best drink evvverrrr because that will probably have to do you, bless your hearts :o)

All in all, there was space to play, wander, and dream. It was ideal.

In fact, the house came with a history for both of my folks and their families. It had once been a rental, and my mother and Grandma Stella had lived there *before* my dad's family went to work for the owner; *then* my mom's family had to move out so Dad's family, the Feltrops, could move in. Grandpa William eventually purchased the four-room home place and had long since passed away, now Grandma Lucy lived there alone. Sadly, Grandma was losing a battle with Alzheimer's and now needed constant attention, so Mom and Dad had come back to help. Now they were both back in their childhood home, along with me and my brother, in Mount Pisgah. Our little sister would show up a year later. Welcome, Angela. And there would be no more moves for our little family.

Eventually the family had to place Grandma Lucy in a care facility. My folks bought the house and land. They got a loan—an American tradition. They drew up plans for an addition for our growing family, added a luxury item—indoor plumbing—and we settled in.

This would be the place where I would grow up, and we still call it home today.

This was also the place where the nightmares set in. Robbing me of sleep. Filling me with dread and fear.

This was where I would meet Jesus, when I was ten, where He not only asked me if I loved Him but if I would "follow" Him. This is where I said, "Yes."

This is where I learned to say prayers and weave stories, adventures, and incredible journeys in my head before sleep would slide in and my foes would return to haunt me.

This was the place … these were the things that would shape me into the woman I would become.

&·~

When it was time for me to begin school, I entered our dusty, rural bus quietly. A bit shy, I preferred to stay in the background. Things had changed, I had changed, since our move to Morris School Road. I now preferred to watch and learn about the people around me before I stepped in close or moved. I guess I was gauging people even then, because I never felt "settled" until I had everyone's personalities slid into a box: safe, not safe, nice, mean, etc. For someone who liked adventure, apparently I didn't like surprises.

As months, seasons, and years rolled by, I somehow managed to create roles for myself on the old school bus.

A peacemaker. "Okay, so Jimmy, you like Fords, and Randy, you like Chevys. But can you pleassssee not holler about which is better? You *both* like trucks so why don't you talk about why owning a truck would be *wayyyy* better than having a car. Okay? However, I agree with Jimmy, Fords are best." Negotiating done ... *check.*

Greeter and safety coordinator. "Hello, Andrea, aren't you Bud's niece? My name is Sherry, and I think you are going to *loveeee* kindergarten. How about we sit up front here? By the way, this is Stephanie, and she's super nice and this is ..." Ensuring little kids didn't drift to the rough bunch and get picked on ... *check.*

The listener and encourager. "Hey, Jimmy how are you and Bert liking living in the country?" "What are your hobbies?" "How did it go at school?" "What's that you are reading?" Allowing them to know we were their new family and letting the other kids know the quiet city boys were cool.

The vigilante. If you did twist the little kids' ears or were mean to the new kid, I was going to be on you! Actually, *actually,* I tried to stay out of it when I was the only member of my family on the bus, *but* once my brother started riding, I was ALL *in.* And sooooo, when the day came that he sat in the back (*despite* what I had told him) and they started picking on him, I took all of my frustration of the past three years with me as I marched to the back of the bus. A scrawny eight-year-old with long, dark, uncombed tresses. (Quite a sight, I am sure, bless my heart.) I didn't EVEN try to talk, because they just laughed at people, including Barney, our bus driver, when anyone told them to quit. I just reached over to where my brother was trying to get away under the seat and I pinched and scratched until I drew blood! Okay, I even think I sound a little scary—yikes!!!! But on that occasion and any similar event that followed, I was never reprimanded. Barney always just let me handle it, never telling me to get back *into* my seat until it was all over and done.

Time does a lot, and we all grew up. Eventually we were all just a big family. Barney retired. Another driver came … and another. And so went my experience with life and my community of friends and neighbors on the yellow peril.

Mom and we kids attended a country church in Crosby. It was small enough that I knew *everybody* there. Well, actually, I only knew those that sat on my side. I loved visiting with the older people, especially Cheryl and Robert's grandma, but maybe not so much the little kids, as I had enough of that at home with my siblings. I also enjoyed the time with my peers and teachers in Sunday School. The music? The music was all vocal and so pretty, with people singing harmonies. Beautiful. Melodious. Serene wellllll okay, Mrs. Meuli might have been a tad louder than necessary, but I did learn to *clearly* hear the alto line as she generally sat a couple of rows behind us. :O)

I *loved* everything about the church: the people, music, and lessons. But NOT the church clothes. Fancy, itchy dresses, uncomfortable shoes, lacy socks that never stayed up, and SOMEONE still needed to help me understand how putting bobby pins and those awful big bows in my hair could become such a painful ordeal. I was thoroughly convinced that my mom was just doing it to torture me!

Anyways church wasn't the problem. The pain of formality— that was. The hair prep stuff that was. The most wearisome thing of all, however, was missing the last fifteen minutes of every Sunday morning Tarzan movie!

Even when I was in elementary school I loved most folks, but I didn't get *real* close to very many, like having a "best-est" friend. I preferred to run with the masses, talk to everybody, and jump in and out of groups OR better yet, go solo. And a lot of the time I did just that.

Alone I could sing, talk, and walk with God up on the hill. As I added years I also added love songs, with lofty dreams filled with expectation and anticipation. The older I became, the more frequent the walks up into my quiet haven became. There I found space to lose the weight of school, peers, and family. There I could just ... be. There I knew I was seen by the One who loved me as I was and knew me best. There my dreams had no limits.

I believed all the Bible stories and everything my teachers had said about Him having great plans for me. With Him, I could step off and pray through today, as well as for the future and the love I hoped one day to find. Those were sweet times, filled with unspoken but heard promises. Those times left me with joy, settling like dew drops in the deep recesses of my heart. And joy is far different from happiness, because it is not temporal but roots down in a soul for extended stays. It walks with you into the darkness and through the nightmares and back into the light of day. It offers hope and brings life despite the harshness of the hour or journey. Whether it is a sunny or stormy day. Whether you are in love or brokenhearted.

Now, love ... Awwwww. Love is something we all dream of and long for. I was no different. That being said, I may have spent more time considering what type of man and marriage I wanted than some of my peers. There was an ideal I longed for but also a list in my heart of things I prayed I'd never have to deal with. My few years of living had already concreted my thoughts regarding everything MY marriage would not be: marred with alcohol, adultery, selfishness, and bitterness. I had heard the stories and witnessed the wounds families endured when those attributes reigned in a home. THAT would not be *my* end and *not* be the shadow that haunted my children. My heart's cry was reaffirmed each year at church camp as I recommitted my soul's desire to not only find love but to find a man of faith to share life's journey with.

Now, you'd think you could find such a specimen at church camp. An eligible, God-fearing man with a sense of humor that reached his eyes, and IF he happened to be ruggedly handsome with some passion and fire, that would be my bonus request IF God asked. Which I wasn't sure He would. LOL

Now while I found boyfriends there, I also lost them soon after, year after year. There was Brian. Curly headed and blond, athletic and blue eyed. And in one week, gone. There was Bob. Redheaded with gray eyes, strong and broad. And in a matter of weeks, gone. The next year there was David, brown hair and eyes, a bit of a cowboy, long and lean. But just like the others, in time, gone. Ten days of camp. Six-day romances and a slow fade. What are kids thinking? What was I thinking? Great Scott! When I was sixteen, I remember crying my eyes out for a week after camp because I had gotten a "Dear Jane" letter. There I was, sitting in the backyard swing, wailing and writing crazy love songs. I even thought I was off my hinges when I looked up and had a vision of someone that looked like an older version of Ike Eisenmann (the boy best known for his role on *Escape to Witch Mountain*—Google him, kiddos) riding on a white horse, coming down the hill toward me around the chicken coop and outdoor toilet.

Who sees stuff like that???

Okay, that did at least make me stop crying, because it was so real and *weird*!

Anyways … I had several years where I was distracted by something at church camp other than what I came for. That being said, our female counselors were always encouraging us to focus on God's plans for our future, which included many discussions on purity, dating, what to look for in a husband, characteristics of a godly man. And let's just face the truth: guys are always an *interesting* topic for teenage girls. As an older youth we'd make pledges annually to pray not just for "a guy" but for the "right guy." So that and Jesus are what I'd be thinking about for *all* of camp UNLESS I got swept up in a summer camp romance.

But as a people watcher, I had already begun gauging the relationships among my peers by the time I hit seventh grade, and I had seen enough to realize I didn't want to add any more drama to my life. I also didn't want to live in the chaos that followed the breakups, five days a week (tears, anger, opinions floating everywhere) with the whole school watching and taking sides! I still had sufficient excitement when I slept with my night terrors. I definitely didn't need to take on more in the light of day. In my mind, love was safer in daydreams and at church camp, where there was a whole bunch of supervision. So I left it there until my senior year, and even then, I came in slow.

2

As my senior year started I was super excited. One, I was almost DONE! Two, since Debbie, my church and school-bus buddy of eleven years, and I both had part-time jobs (she at a local restaurant and me at the Nautilus Center), we only had to go to school part time! Three, this meant we often got to drive. Okay, Debbie got to drive, as I still had not taken the test to get my driver's license. (Go ahead, I heard you say it: slacker. And, yes, I was :o)

On my lucky mornings – NO BUS. Mom would drive me up the road to meet Deb by Little Indian Creek, and then she and I would head to town in her family's BIG ol white ride. The only problem with it wasn't even the car's fault. I was a skinny mess, almost six feet tall comprised mostly of legs. Debbie was a cute lil' blonde standing about five foot two. In order for her to reach the pedals AND see over the dash, she had to slide the front seat ALL THE WAY forward, which meant I could almost rest my chin on my knees! (That's a little bit of an exaggeration, but not much.) Oh well, it was a minor inconvenience to endure for all the independence gained!

We thought we had finally arrived. Looking back, I have no clue what we thought we had arrived *to,* as getting a license, job, and senior ring doesn't equate AT ALL with becoming an adult. But we were teenagers; we thought we knew everything and *we* had the world by the tail, so somehow in our minds, not riding the school bus with the "little kids" meant we were grown up.

Debbie and I had been riding the same bus since we started school, but it was our relationship at church that had kept us close as we had gotten older. We didn't actually have a *whole* lot in common besides church and a love for country living. She was nineteen and dating; she liked older guys (than high school) and beards (yuck)! I was seventeen. I not only wasn't dating, but I didn't even go to school games, dances, social events, or uptown on the weekends with friends. And while I wasn't sure what I liked, I knew it was NOT beards. ANYWAYSSSS at church, you don't usually talk about that stuff. There we were just two more back-wood girls meeting under a small white steeple. There you loved everybody and every one spoke to one another, even kids you might not hang out with in the halls at school. But come Sunday, you were family.

My senior year started out great, but my classes were all so easy that I was soon bored. Two of my hours were home economics classes, where they taught us about marriage, cooking, and managing a home. Those were actually things I wanted to know, as I knew I would use them in the future. Sadly, all Mrs. V ever spent much time talking about was how quickly she would get a divorce if she had $300. WOW! Now that was NOT something I hoped to know anything about in the future.

Debbie wasn't particularly fond of school either, so on the days we didn't work, we took advantage of an open campus to go enjoy the great outdoors. To embrace our youthful energy. To *walk* in the sunshine. Okay, in reality, we were skipping school. Let it be noted—we always pulled into the parking lot and talked about what we should do before we left and headed to the trails at the lake or out to B-Rock to hike. (Oh dear, I can hear it now! All you parents go ahead and say, "That is awful." It wasn't good on our part, but neither was the concept of an Open Campus OR Designated Smoking Areas for students. Let's just say a lot of things weren't right. I'll own mine. Sorrrrry, Mom.)

Sooo Debbie was my childhood bus and church buddy, and now you know she was also my class-cutting buddy. But we hadn't actually hung out at school for a year. Our high school was pretty large, and while everyone else seemed to have stepped into the teen scene, becoming more socially acclimated, I had not. Looking back, I guess I may have looked forlorn sitting on the front steps of the auditorium alone, but I never felt lonely. I was content with my company, and quite frankly I didn't like to hear about the drama, drunkenness, or other stuff that had gone on the weekend before or that they were planning for the upcoming weekend. I preferred to keep everybody at face value so my intentional segregation was my way of relaying, "Please don't share your private junk."

Actually, I started embracing that attitude before high school, as I had stopped eating in the lunchroom after fifth grade because I got so anxious every time someone mentioned sneaking, cheating, or hating. Remember, I am the girl that had terrors almost nightly while other people rested and slept. I saw no need to watch a soap opera unfold at noon; the only thing I had an interest in opening on lunch break was a soda and a box of Wheat Thins. That was about as much as I could handle.

So now you know. I had "friends," but I was a loner, a loner sitting in the sun with some crazy, frizzy curl to her auburn hair and unrealized but concrete dreams in her heart. By my senior year, I could be found (okay at least on the days I was at school) seated on the auditorium steps reading history books or romances, which are nothing alike, but hey, that was who I was.

After school I would take the bus home until I finally decided to get my driver's license. I actually could have gotten my permit at fourteen and been driving alone at sixteen, but I had a little problem. It wasn't that I had lost my love of independent adventures; it was just that my dad's training technique to equip me to drive had left me shocked and stunned.

You think I'm exaggerating? You take someone who has never driven anything besides a three-wheeler and put her in a clutch vehicle. Park it halfway up a steep incline. Tell her where she'll end up (in the Shourd's and Anderson's front yard) if she doesn't manage the clutch, gas, and shifting correctly, THEN YOU SEE if she opts to try that *knowing* that not only is it going to be embarrassing rolling into her friend's ditch and front lawn, but her peers will have plenty of entertainment as they catch her taking a heated, *colorful* tongue-lashing from her dad!! Yuppp! That is why I had been saying *no* to learning to drive. Now, two months into school, I was ready to bite the bullet and just get it done.

I had also decided it was time I started trying to become more active in the school program and clubs, as our school counselor had JUST met with me to tell me that active/leadership stuff mattered on college applications. Suddenly just graduating wasn't sufficient; I needed to add interaction in social activities. Ughhh! So, in I jumped, willingly but not terribly excited. FHA (for young homemakers). DECA (for those in the work program). FTA (Future Teachers of America). Girls' Ensemble. Choir (my one long-time steady). For someone who didn't feel the need to stay socially engaged, it was a overkill, but sometimes you just have to do what needs doin', so in I went.

Several of those clubs had social events, and it wasn't until after I was elected as an officer that I found out officers were *expected* to go and NOT ONLY GO but go early and stay late to set up and clean up. Come October, I nervously went to DECA's fall hayride event. The one thing that made it easier for me was the fact that it was out by my church camp and not far from where Debbie and I would hike, so it kinda felt like "home" to me there. And as it is not my nature to skip out on responsibilities (except, apparently, school itself), I tried to calm the loud voice in my head that kept asking me, even as I reached in to grab my jacket out of the car, if I didn't think I felt sick.

Instead of bailing, I inhaled and exhaled and "stepped away from the car." (Can you hear it? It sounds like the officer on COPS, "Step away from the car. Move forward. Slowly and *nobody* gets hurt." But it is just the voice in my head encouraging me that this won't kill me and I am surely NOT going to die. LOL) It really wasn't that bad once the supplies showed up and we had the stuff to actually set up. I liked helping out, and hot dogs and chili are kind of no-brainers, so it was easy and left me with time to catch up and actually "visit" with people I'd been going to school with for twelve years but hadn't actually talked to in a long time. I spent a lot of time talking to one young man in particular, Gordy. He had actually been my boyfriend off and on throughout elementary school, and now he was here, serving as our recently elected club president. We were both, even as children, a little "old for our years," as my mom would say, and it was refreshing to find that he was just as easy to talk to all these years later as he had been back when we had played army ten years earlier.

We were still visiting after we, ate and it seemed natural when we loaded up for the hayride that we sat next to each other. I don't remember much after that, except for what I can't deny, because someone had a camera and it ended up in our yearbook. (I AIN'T even lying! Ask Gordy. I doubt he knows either.) I can remember being kissed and then hay—not under us but all on top of us! Honestly! I don't remember how we got in the predicament we were in when they snapped that photo, but we won't EVER be able to forget it. Bless our hearts :o)

Gordy and I started "dating" after that. Our elementary school peers seemed elated to see us reunited after an eight-year break-up LOL. (Can you really call it a relationship when we still needed our moms' signatures on homework packets???) Well regardless, I guess we all did, because even my mom was ecstatic—as she had always said, he was the cutest boy and had told him so IN FRONT OF ME at our fourth-grade open house event! (Probably didn't bother him, as I am sure it sounded like a compliment, but it embarrassed me plum to death!) Well, he was polite, with wavy black hair and sincere brown eyes so that would qualify for cute.

So here we go. I am part of a couple.

He treats me wonderfully. Guards me. Respects me. Encourages me. Makes plans for us and our future after graduation as we talk on the phone nightly until my mom makes me hang up and go to bed. James Brinkley, a broadly built, strong football player who had gone to primary school with us and was a common friend, was as happy about it as my mom. He enjoyed teasing me about Gordy and I being childhood sweethearts and happy endings in DECA class every day after lunch. You know it's just odd to see jocks excited about romance in general, and then, to have several of my country boy friends celebrating Gordy's and my courtship, that was just unfathomable to me, *but* they did. And I didn't mind it, as it was our reality.

In fact, EVERYBODY said it was perfect—including me. I was a tad bit taller than him, but I was taller than most of the guys, and it didn't seem to bother him. And when I wrecked my (new to me but slightly used) Grand Prix (with a sunroof, leather seats, and power windows!!! Okay that wasn't standard stuff back in the day, so be excited about my upgrades, please :o) ... ANYWAYSSSS, I wrecked my car while my mom and siblings were out of town and Gordy was ready to run to my rescue.

The only trouble was that this was before *everybody* had cell phones, and so when I did wake up from my little nap (I took a bit of a hit on the head when I crashed) and someone FINALLY came down our road where I'd been walking it and could take me home, it was getting late. BY the time I got hold of Gordy and filled him in, I heard tires slowing on gravel outside and looked out to see dad pulling in. Yikes!!! I immediately began anticipating his heated, unedifying remarks so I told Gordy not to come and hung up.

Now was the time I was going to need to pull out some fast, clear explanations, *not* invitations. And Lord knows I wasn't going to need any witnesses to the tongue lashing I was fixin' to get! Not that my Dad would have ever hurt me. I just had always hated disappointing people, especially my Dad.

Let it be noted that on this occasion my dad was wonderful! Dad said nothing. He argued with me a little as he retraced our road back to where *I said* my car was. He had just come that way and had not seen my vehicle, so *he* was certain I was mistaken. I was smart enough not to argue; I just kept telling him it was in the ditch alongside the road where 'washboards' formed after it rained really hard. (That means the dirt road would just wash out enough that it got REALLY bumpy.) I forgot to mention that it was actually standing on its nose in a DEEP ditch. (Who knew that was there? We'd lived there forever, but no one ever mowed around that little creek with all those shrubs. NOW I knew those shrubs were trees and that ditch was deep enough to stand up and hide a fourteen-foot-long car.)

Needless to say, when Dad saw the car he got quiet and I got tense, waiting, but his frustration *never* surfaced. Actually, my Dad was almost mute as he watched a neighbor pull it out and we followed the bent piece of wreckage home. For whatever reason, he never got around to giving me the fussing I expected. So, I came through the wreck and the reckoning unscathed, except I was on foot again, bumming rides or begging to use Mom's car.

But back to romance. Gordy had taken me on one date after the hayride, and I was a little less than comfortable and not at all sure what we would do with that much one-on-one time. Gordy didn't have a problem, but that just created *more* problems, as I had not dated before and the whole dating thing was a bit overwhelming for me. Then I had had the wreck. And we both had jobs. And when he asked me out again, I suggested he come to our house. Since we'd been talking about getting married, he might as well get to know my family. By this time, everyone in our DECA class was anticipating him giving me his senior ring any day (which was a big deal in the eighties.) We were all full of anticipation; it had become a class-wide romance in which everyone seemed to have opinions about and wanted to be included in, including Mrs. Moseley, our teacher.

When Gordy arrived, we immediately headed up into the hills behind the house. My stomach was full of butterflies. November was winding down, and it was a cool, beautiful day. We hiked and visited all the way up to the new pond, which was set off back into the woods. Picking a sunny place on the far west bank, we sat on freshly fallen leaves under the bare arbor limbs. It was perfect. My favorite time of year. My favorite place. My favorite guy. Kissing my favorite guy. Then we started talking, and I could hear the seriousness and knew it was coming. But something was wrong.

Gordy was holding my hand and talking about the future we had been planning. Just as we did on the phone. It was sweet, all that I had imagined. But then my stomach went from butterflies to knots, and my mind disengaged from what was being said as I tried to understand what was going on in my head and heart. The next thing I knew, I felt like I was helplessly stuck in one of my nightmares. As I saw him slip the ring toward me, unexplainable panic rose within me. Interrupting the moment, I spoke.

The words that came out were as much of a shock to him as they were to me. "No."

Totally confused, I shook my hand free, trying to understand what was going on. Gordy was asking questions I couldn't understand. Standing, I looked at him once, completely muddled in my mind, then quickly began the trek back home. Gordy stayed with me, walking quietly after he realized I wasn't going to stop and talk. I didn't make a sound; it felt like one of my dreams, where I am thinking and speaking but just can't be heard, so I just hurried through the woods and down the hill in silence.

Ten minutes later, when we were passing his dark green pickup, he slowed down, no longer at my side. I kept walking, up the front porch steps and into the living room, and plopped down on the carpet facing the door. He paused momentarily at his truck but followed me in, acknowledging everyone before he sat down just as quietly on the floor across from me, facing me. I had not said a word or acknowledged anyone when I came in but he had. See, I told you, even in the midst of "my chaos," he was still polite!

I had flat-lined. I sat very quiet and still. Quiet is also what settled over the living room after we entered as my mom, my brother, and our company had stopped visiting when I rushed in. They were staring at me before Gordy came in. Then at him as he entered the scene. Then back and forth between us. I could feel Gordy's eyes upon me, piercing the distance trying to read my mind and call me out, but I *didn't even* have a clue what I was thinking, so good luck with that! I looked at him but had no voice, absolutely nothing to say, so my eyes finally just locked on the ground between us. He too had now become silent.

My mom eventually tried to reinitiate the conversation they had been having *before* we came in, probably to cover up the awkward stillness, but neither my brother nor Mark, a family friend, seemed interested in it any longer. They simply looked from one to the other of us. Awkward. It was soooooo awkward that Gordy stood back up and told me he would call later, said a courteous goodbye to the others, and left.

I continued to sit locked up and incapable of even speaking until Mark left. Mark was some years older than me, but my mom was insistent that he liked me. (Someone tell me how is it that you go from NO guys hanging around to having spares???) But that wasn't the problem, or at least that's what I thought, until he also left, and then I got a scolding from my mom for being rude to both of them. I don't remember anything else but going to bed early, completely unsure of what had happened, still housing this twisting inside my gut that insisted I couldn't have said, "Yes."

I thought all the questions were over as I left for school Monday and I escaped my mother's scrutiny; *however,* I didn't know I would get to school and find a dozen friends ANGRY with me! "How could you be so stupid?" "Don't you realize you two were meant to be together?" "I cannot believe you are going to hurt him like that! Are you going to fix it?" So many opinions and so much unwanted advice and concern over what I had done and what I should do. So many questions. So many people informing me about how he was taking it. *Day after day.* Class upon class, but ESPECIALLY in our DECA class, which thankfully Gordy and I did not have during the same hour.

I wish I could have just fixed it. But I not only couldn't fix it; I couldn't feel—anything. For him or for me. I didn't have an excuse. I was perplexed as much as they were. I was also numb and could not find a thought, a dream, or even a nightmare that would shake *any* emotion back to my life.

3

And so it went for three weeks and into December. My brain wasn't any better at letting things drop than theirs, and so I just tried to stay busy. And then, on the nineteenth of December, Debbie and I elected to go hiking on a WEEKEND rather than a school day :o). After changing into sweatshirts, jeans, and comfortable shoes, we took off in her car to B-Rock out past Camp Wyldewood. Away from the world, climbing up and over hills, we talked a little about this, and I even talked a little to her about THAT thing that had happened on the hill with Gordy, and as I voiced it, I got to thinking: I really didn't have a good excuse—I didn't have *any* excuse—for locking up on Gordy. We did seem like the perfect pair, so maybe I was as stupid as everybody kept saying and I just needed to go and say I was sorry and see if he would take me back.

When we got back to the car, Deb drove me straight to the Pizza Hut on Race Street, where Gordy worked. His coworker said he couldn't talk now and was working until like five. So, I said I would just leave him a note on his truck. With that done, we headed back downtown to kill some time. Now as we were still living in the "cruising era," it was easy to see who was out running around that you wanted to visit with. 'Cause that's the way "cruising" works. You go between two points, in Searcy's case between Sonic and the courthouse in order to check out who's driving or who's parked in some parking lot, and then you stop before or after you loop the courthouse. Anyway, cruising back and forth without stopping was what I thought we were going to do, until Debbie spotted Robert, a boy from church, in the Piggly Wiggly parking lot. (And no, I didn't make that up; it is an actual grocery store we still have scattered throughout the south :o)

After we pulled in, I understood why Debbie had been sooo excited about stopping to talk with Robert. You see, I *knew* it couldn't have just been visiting with Robert because we had just seen Robert a couple of hours previously. And Robert had been flirting with us every Sunday at church since we were fourteen! (You gotta love his persistence! LOL) But Debbie wasn't interested in him, then or now. Nooooo, Deb was stopping where Robert was because of the other guy that was there, leaning against a gray Camaro, whom Robert was talking TO. However at this point, it didn't matter to me how she chose to spend the hour or so; we were going to need to wait in town. I was back to that numb thing and trying to fight my way through to stay the course until five.

Thankfully, she had parked a couple of spaces down from them and exited to go visit where they were standing so I had time and now I had space to think. As it was a warm and sunny day, I reached over and turned the key in order to roll my window down. Resting my arms across my knees, I laid my head down, once again lost in thought. I could not get myself reconciled! I didn't even know what was still trying to give me fits! Was it my heart or my head? What was my deal anyway! There was no legit argument against Gordy. Spent and strained, I leaned back, propping my elbows on my knees, which were still soooo close to my face, as Deb had not scooted the seat back. Ughhhh!

My legs were cramping a bit from the hike. My brain was locked up and my heart froze. I had no idea what I was thinking IF I was thinking at all. My head seemed to be cramping up as well and THAT I couldn't seem to do a thing to fix. But as for those leg cramps … unwilling to forfeit my isolation and get out of the car, I leaned back, wiggling my feet and rubbing my head. Oh, to have everything ease back in line and conform to normal.

I was completely lost in thought, but the silence didn't last long before a familiar voice broke through.

"Hey!" It was Robert. Ever a flirt, but *right now* I definitely didn't want to play. I didn't even turn my head, which is probably why he repeated himself. "Hey." This time I turned slightly toward him, not bothering to hide the fact that I was more than a little annoyed. My jaw was SET and my eyebrows arched as my gaze swung around. But today Robert wasn't intimidated. Nor was he going to be shooed off so easily; *in fact*, he started giving ME orders.

"Sherry, get out of the car." WHAT!!! I could not believe my ears! He might have been a year or two older than me, and we might have been church friends for seven years, *but* I had four to five inches on him in height! And I didn't want to sass and play verbal games at this moment—after all these years of that nonsense, you would think he would be able to tell when I was up for his shenanigans, and today was definitely a NOT! The fact was that I was having a battle with myself, which I didn't want interrupted by anyone FOR anything. PERIOD.

But even as I tried to turn away, he spoke again! "Sherry, just unfold your long self and show this guy how tall you are." That was the first time I noticed that anybody was with him. Knowing that since he had an audience I wasn't going to have *any* peace until I had fulfilled his request, I sat up, pushed open the car door, and "unfolded." Then I turned to face my annoying friend and his friend as they laughed at Robert's wit.

There he stood, Debbie's Camaro man, a nice brown mullet, a cocky smile, and an arrogant attitude. Debbie's kinda guy. I could understand why she stopped to look, but that boy was a hot mess. I could see it when we pulled in, and now, standing near him, I found myself more annoyed by him than Robert—and he hadn't even said anything! Well, Robert could be a nuisance, but he was my friend. I wouldn't pick this guy to be friendly with. No, sir! I didn't like messes. But if you need to hear me say something positive, well, I did like his red and black flannel shirt and his brown hiking boots with red shoe strings and … yuppp that's all. That would have been it!

So now it seemed the party had moved over to where we stood, and there went my quiet, and just when I thought it couldn't frustrate me more, yeah, it did. Because now came the invite from "Mr. Joe-Cool" wanting to know if we wanted to go for a ride.

I answered for all of us, "No, we are meeting someone." None of us needed his kind of trouble. Robert definitely didn't need his influence, and Debbie needed to back it up before she got more than she could handle. With my thoughts firm, I had said it: "No."

But Debbie trumped in, overriding me. "Sure we will. Sherry, we have plenty of time to make a couple of loops before then." *Gosh!* This was inconvenient and going to push my timetable! But if Debbie was going, so was I, because I needed to make sure we were back in time to be at the Pizza Hut at five. Besides that, I didn't trust this guy, or even my friend with this guy to remember my appointment.

My mind was clicking away now, and I was hoping Robert might help me be the voice of reason and diffuse the situation.

However, I soon found I had another issue rising up before that one could even be resolved. As in disbelief, I heard the mullet man "dismiss" Robert as we were walking back toward their cars.

What in the world! Who does that?

He did. That's who. Circling his ride, he told Robert he would see him later.

I hadn't even had time to come up with another full thought before he spoke again, telling us both to sit up front. Mind you, it was like a 1968 (or something) Camaro—a small sports car with bucket seats and a slim console in the middle. Quickly I looked over and, oh-no! There's a glimmer in Deb's eyes. *Dang!* I knew her well enough to know what that meant. She was looking forward to sitting on that console and rubbing elbows with him, and this simply would not do.

What do I do? I needed a minute to think, but there wasn't half of that! So when she opened our door (because he of course didn't), I moved quickly, almost pushing her aside to get in the middle and perch on that console seat! As I congratulated myself for making a six-foot wall between them, I could feel the heat of her stare on me, yet I didn't move. He quickly slid it in gear and off we took. My location made eye contact between them almost impossible. Yes!!! And thank the Lord my brain had engaged again!

I was focused and for the first time in a month, feeling something. Okay, it might have been anger, but it *was* an emotion, and my brain *was* in gear. In fact, it was working so well I did a highly effective job keeping ALL our conversations where I needed them. Work. Songs. Favorite music groups. School. Short and sweet answers.

That being said, once again, I was what my mother would have considered rude. But it had to be done. And now, thankfully, this ride was almost done. He slowed up and rolled back in to the Piggly Wiggly parking lot. That's when I squared back around and found I had another problem. Debbie was hot, and by hot, I mean really mad! Her face was flushed, and her blue eyes were dark! When she slung open the door, I thought, *I am not going to just need a ride to Pizza Hut. I am going to have to find myself a ride home if I don't hustle, because she is fixing to leave my butt in this parking lot!'*

Sliding off the console as quickly as I could, I had one leg out the door when he said my name. "Sherry."

I quickly turned back toward him, and that was when he just laid one on me! Kissed me RIGHT on the lips! After one trip up Race Street! If I hadn't been in such a hurry to catch Debbie I'd have slapped him back into last week! But I was out and gone!

Deb was leaning against her car door with her arms crossed as I hustled over, reaching tentatively for the door handle. It did not look good. Would all our years of being friends be enough to get us past this? I hoped we—

Once again my thoughts are interrupted. "Hey, can you get me the free two-month membership cards for karate and Nautilus you said you had with you?" Ughh … I'd mentioned them when we were on the safe "work topic," and he asked how much stuff cost. I was killing time and talking too much apparently. I just make messes, and here was another one. I just needed him to go away! But he stood waiting between the two vehicles.

Oh, my word! What to do?? I looked helplessly at Debbie to make sure if I stepped away from the car she wasn't going to take off. When she turned and quirked her eyebrow at me, I took that as a "do it quick" and reached in, grabbed the card from my purse, hurried over to where he waited, and handed it to him. Then I fairly raced back to where the car sat WITH the motor running and in gear. She was ready to go.

4

It was a bit before five o'clock, and I wondered if she would still be willing to take me back to see Gordy, but I wasn't going to say ANYTHING. When she turned east onto Race Street toward Pizza Hut, I leaned back, relieved, and began trying to remember where I had been before Robert had interrupted me almost an hour before. But upon our arrival, I found it was all in vain. Gordy was already gone, and after a loop looking for him in town, we took off to the dirt roads that led to our homes. I didn't know what else to do. He didn't have a phone in his apartment. And I actually didn't know where he lived, so that was done for the moment. Maybe he was still indignant about my response and attitude? Maybe he had moved on? Our mutual friends hadn't mentioned that or eased up on me.

The truth was I just didn't know what he thought because I hadn't bothered to try and find out by asking him. And apparently, we were not going to talk about it today.

For now, I was just grateful Debbie was a good enough friend to still give me a ride back to my house, even if it was reallllyyyy quiet. Oddly my mind had slipped back into neutral.

Once again, I wasn't thinking or feeling anything.

I was thankful for two things going into Monday morning. One, we were out of school for Christmas break, and surely within fourteen days, Gordy would forgive me, as that had always seemed to be his nature with everyone. Two, I had a job to take my mind off of things, and the next night I was hard at it, serving as a fitness instructor at the Nautilus center. I enjoyed my job, and it usually kept me busy enough not to be bored while giving me just enough time to socialize with the friends I had made there since my brother had started taking taekwondo three years earlier. My brother, sister, and mom were all there as well, working out in the karate arena. World champion black belts after the Las Vegas competition in November, they were volunteer instructors under Mr. Brown, my boss.

Now I NEVER went in to the workout arena, because I DID NOT take karate. I'd been there and watched for three years. I even knew the forms and could offer advice about their technique. I loved to watch and cheer during competitions, but I had never ever actually taken a class. Three years of being there, three times a week, and I'd *never even* been on the floor. I'd never been in a gi. Never been in there to warm up and get all sweaty. I'd never wanted to take my turn getting kicked or blocking punches. And while it looked like fun and I was pretty sure I might enjoy it, I'd never tried busting a single board.

This girl liked to read, cross-stitch, crochet, and hike in the cooler seasons. I did NOT like to sweat, and everybody who knew me knew that. I was great at visiting, instructing, and greeting but not at kicking, spinning, or both at the same time! I think that calls for some level of coordination, and I'm not sure how much of that I was gifted with at birth, and heaven knows I had not worked on developing it :o) Besides, I could shoot. I could shoot really, *really* well—so I always told folks that that was my preferred method of self-defense. Hence why Mr. Brown put me to work in the Nautilus arena. If he couldn't make any money off of me on the karate instruction side, then he would use the time I was sitting around waiting on my family to help him earn money on the other side. :o) Checking people in. Charting their repetitions. Setting their weights, etc.

And that's exactly what I was doing when my Piggly Wiggly guy came in. I knew his name, which would have been a bit odd, since Robert only said it once and Debbie had not broken her vow of silence on our way home the previous night to chit-chat about him. It would have been odd, except that I had heard it Sunday night, when one of my classmates called me. Apparently, someone had seen Mr. Camaro-man kiss me, or they had seen me with him, and they said that's why Gordy wasn't there when I came by and wouldn't call. The odd thing was that I received not just that one call but also another call from one of my out-of-town friends from the karate studio warning me of what type of guy Lenny was.

Can we pause to applaud the social highway network way back before smart phones and instant notifications? Back *before* all that, in *less than* four hours, my peers were fully aware of the fact that I had *been* to the Pizza Hut and *where* I went after and *who* I was with for maybe thirty minutes, and they *even* knew about the kiss! You see, you really don't have to have Snapchat and Facebook to know what is going on.

So not only did my peers know my activity, but *apparently* everybody presumed I was too stupid or naïve to see what kind of guy he was. And once again, *everybody* was in a tizzy at me because of the way I was treating Gordy and EVERYTHING was my fault.

Maybe it was, but *nobody* was asking or believing my side of the story, and *now* I knew that his Camaro's presence in front of the studio was *not* going to help validate my story. In fact, to make matters worse, my work location was almost directly across the road from the Pizza Hut, and since guys KNOW cars, I knew it was only a matter of minutes until my sphere of friends would know that Lenny (Mr. Romeo) was where I was.

Crazy how guys always identify people by their vehicle. But yuppp, his slick silver ride parked in the front of my place of employment was going to guarantee more calls of caution and reasoning. Wonderful. *Not*!

I was immediately annoyed, but attempting to be as professional as possible, I took him to Mr. Brown's office so he could talk with him before the beginner's class started. I was hopeful the commitment would put him off, as rumor had it commitments did. But ten minutes later, Mr. Brown came by congratulating me on recruiting a new member as he passed through to class, pausing just long enough to remind me to "smile" as he headed in to teach. My mom was right I was rude. But right now, my rudeness didn't bother me. His presence in my home away from home did.

Finishing up a client, I paused in front of one of the hall windows to watch as he lined up with the other students on the karate floor and began warm-ups. What on earth was he was doing here? Once again, I found myself becoming angry. I felt almost like a prisoner in my own house. What kind of guy just does stuff like that, kissing girls he just met and then just showing up acting so nonchalantly, as if he hadn't done anything wrong???

Coming to myself, I realized I was staring and he had caught me. Flustered and embarrassed, I headed back to work. An hour later, he was in the weight area, asking me where to start. It looked like he was going to do a trial on both sides of the fitness area. Great! And to top it off, I was the only one working the floor, so there was no way to get out of doing what must come next—weighing, measuring (chest, biceps, waist, hips, thighs), and charting his personal info. I went a thousand shades of red just thinking about it. That made me mad, and even as I was trying to work myself through it, Mr. Brown passed through on his way to the next class and gave me "The Look," which said, "I don't know what YOU think you are doing, but YOU are on my time, and that's a potential client. Do it and do it right. And smile." Yeah, when your eyes know how to talk, you don't need words. Mr. Brown didn't need words. I heard him loud and clear.

My A personality kicked into overdrive, and I set to the task at hand. It wasn't as if I hadn't measured plenty of boys and men before, but I was sooooo uncomfortable reaching around measuring his chest and thighs. I wouldn't guarantee any of his numbers were correct, but they were what I saw as quickly as I could touch the tape around upon itself.

Then we were off to the first machine. Explain its use and purpose. Find the correct weight. Count ten to fifteen reps. Record it. Next. The second machine went more quickly, but when it was done and recorded, he didn't move. Instead he said he needed a towel. I abruptly pointed to where they were by the front desk as I moved over to prep the next machine. Lo and behold, there was Mr. Brown AGAIN! I thought he'd gone to class, but NOPE! And this time he was going to use words.

"Sherry," he said in a friendly manner but full of meaning, "be nice to our customers."

Shoot! I had never been reprimanded, and now I had just made my third strike in one afternoon. I knew what he meant: smile and be nice. And so here I go, pasting on a pleasant attitude and plastic smile. The problem is I'm not good at lying OR faking anything! It didn't help to turn around and see Lenny smiling at me.

Inwardly fuming but with a smile on my face, as well as another stupid blushing episode, I headed over to grab him a towel. Halfway there he stopped me. "I don't want one of your towels. I have one in my car."

Wonderful, I thought. I wouldn't have to wait on him after all. Yet even as I turned back around toward him, he continued, "If you'll go get it for me, my car is unlocked, and it's in the driver's seat."

I didn't need a minute to have my next thought because I KNOW ... I KNOW you *didn't* just tell ME to go fetch YOUR stuff!

Ohhhhh but he had. And now he was saying to grab everything out of the seat, because he'd even left his wallet there.

My smile was fixed. My hazel eyes had gone green in a full-blown storm. My body was now taut with emotion. After so many days of numbness, everything in me was alive and raging. I was fit to be tied as I walked through the lobby and outside to get "Mr. Casanova's" junk!

Opening his door quickly hoping to grab and go before the streets made record of me in his car *again* I was halted as I reached down toward the front seat. There was his towel and wallet but also a floral arrangement in a vase with a red rose in it. I thought I was going to be sick. My guy friend who had called earlier had schooled me on the playboy that Lenny was alleged to be. He had also faithfully given me an abbreviated list of the girls Lenny had recently dated and dumped. And NOW here he was flirting and bossing me around before he went out on his way to do WHATEVER it was he did with other girls!

How in the world could anybody who knew me think that I, *of all people*, would take up with that sort of guy over Gordy! Yet that's exactly what they believed. Nobody could conceive that I had not been swept away by him. In those few seconds, as I stood half in and half out of his car, I was furious. I was even madder at him than I had been the night before when he took liberties with me.

Grabbing his towel and wallet, I SLAMMED his door to and went back in. Dropping his wallet under the counter, I strode into the Nautilus arena and unprofessionally tossed him his towel as I went to set up his next machine.

He stood up, wiping his forehead off as he approached the next stop on our circuit. "Where is the rest of my stuff?" he asked nicely enough, but I wasn't feeling nice.

I responded curtly, hoping to appear busy and intentionally making sure my face wasn't visible to Mr. Brown.

"Your wallet is under the counter. That's where we are told to keep things for safety reasons."

"Well, didn't I have anything else in the front seat?" Great Scott! Were we really going to have to go there???

Extremely put off at having a Romeo beat his own drum, I replied tartly as I stiffly motioned him toward the next machine. "The only other thing in the driver's seat was flowers. I saw no need to bring your girlfriend's stuff in here."

Then, looking at me in shock, he responded, "But those are for you."

Awwww shoot! Did my heart skip a beat? I half-turned, thinking he was having fun at my expense. He was smiling but it wasn't *that* kind of smile. Then I blushed *again*. Then he was talking and walking up to me. He touched my hand. And it was stupid! And I *knew* it, but my world rolled over. I could still hear the echo of all of my friend's comments about his lifestyle in my head, but I found I lacked the power or will to stop myself from shyly smiling back at him.

Then in that moment, I noticed something odd. The battle within me that began on that day I sat on the hill with Gordy had ended. I was at rest again.

Finishing his circuit, we didn't have much time to talk as the floor filled up with other clients, and I went between them all setting machines and marking reps. But before he left, we had a date for Christmas evening, and this time when I went to his car, I did not walk out alone.

And this time when he kissed me, I kissed him back.

5

I don't remember much about that Christmas. In fact, I believe that was the first year I did not use my sister's significant age difference to coerce my parents into getting up early so we could open gifts. I don't remember anything I even got. I don't remember the family reunions, save that I was at the Feltrops' reunion, at Aunt Mary and Uncle Ken-Ken's, when Lenny came to pick me up.

I couldn't have planned it better. If he needed intimidation to NOT try something stupid and run over my heart *after* being worked over in karate class by my siblings and mom, then by all means let's go to my tall, barrel-chested, imposing dad. All my guy friends and most of my girlfriends thought my dad was intimidating, and at this shindig I had two uncles to go alongside my dad, and one of those was my Uncle Bud! Good luck with that! Uncle Bud makes my dad look and sound almost angelic. And while I appreciate my family's sense of humor, that's MY normal, so I was a bit apprehensive that Lenny might bolt, maybe even before our date, *but* since everyone had said he wouldn't stick around anyway, we might as well get it figured out.

I was intentionally not watching for him. Trying to remember to hold my guard and be cautious as I realized I had not been in control of myself at all since that first night at the karate studio or the next two nights he was there. Sooooo my uncles were the ones who were shouting through the house when someone saw him pull in. Shyly I edged out to meet him. He did look good in an ecru sweater with a deer across the chest *and* tight blue jeans *and* those hiking boots *and* that mullet! (There are some of you reading this that need to cut me some slack. The mullet was "all that" in the early eighties. We were *all* about the hair! LOL) But anyways he looked good—somehow he always looked good. I will give it to him—he had some nice hair! And the kiss he gave me as he pulled me toward where he reclined up against his car was the onlyyyy gift I remember getting that day.

As we began the walk into the house, I was wondering how it would all pan out. Lenny was five-eleven. My uncles and dad were edging about six inches on him, and when they spoke, the walls seemed to rattle as their voices were very deep and prone to be very loud. I was wincing a little as we stepped up on the porch, as the proof of *volume* was audible even though we had two doors left to open before we were inside. Opening the final door for me, we both exhaled before stepping in. Now for the test. Could he handle my family?

In we walked, from the screened-in sun porch and through the utility room straight into Aunt Mary's dining room and kitchen, which always seemed to smell like someone had just fried bacon. (How did they do that without a scentsy? LOL) Cousins and family members were loitering anywhere and everywhere. I opted to skip most of them as I wanted him to meet the two that were going to cause him the hardest time up front: my dad and my Uncle Bud. I made the introductions, and he didn't flinch as he shook hands and Uncle Bud started the interrogation.

Where you going? When will you be home? You know her curfew? Off they went, unloading questions without always allowing him time even to respond as they gave instructions. I knew they were messing with him. I just hoped he did.

It seemed like forever before I could start saying goodbyes, and we began easing out of the kitchen back onto the porch for a getaway. Once outside, all he said was something about my whole family being tall, and he swung open my door (that's more like it) and in I slid. As he came around and entered his side, he suggested I not sit so far over, and when I scooted over, he leaned in and locked his lips onto mine. Merry Christmas to me! I thought the whole world must have stopped, but I think it was just mine, as he already had the car in reverse and was backing out of the drive before my vision cleared. Then off we went.

I don't think I had any idea where we were going until he asked me if I had seen *Animal House* as we were pulling into the drive-in. I hadn't. I also hadn't been to the drive-in since I was in third grade, and all I remembered about that trip was Mom sitting with Carolyn Kurck, our neighbor, on the tailgate of our old truck while we six kids played chase and made daisy chains. I was quite sure this would be different.

After pulling into a spot, he asked if I wanted to share popcorn (Yes! Who doesn't want popcorn at a movie!!) and a Coke and then off he went. I waited. Then I got nervous. Then I decided I should go to the restroom before it got dark. Then I came back and waited some more. Okay, it might not have been a long time, but I was getting more fidgety by the minute! In fact, he gave me so much time, I got to thinking, what was the movie he'd said we were coming to see? I was almost positive it was *not* a nice movie. I also realized I had a problem, because I was a nice girl, a nice girl who is a poor liar. So when he returned and was settling in and telling me about the movie, I just said, "I don't go to movies like these, R-rated ones." Then I waited.

He didn't get mad. He just laughed and said he'd seen it before and would cover my eyes or "distract me" when the not-so-appropriate parts came on. And he did.

We talked as the movie started up, and we started on that popcorn, but before long I was getting my eyes covered *all the time,* and he suggested we should go to the back seat. His explanation was that we would be more comfortable and I wouldn't have to see all that "stuff." He said it. I believed it. Sooooo we did it. And since he had said "comfortable," I took him at his word and took off my shoes (sorry, but that's what this country girl calls comfort). Tossing them into the front floorboard, they knocked over the rest of our soda. Oops. I thought he'd be upset about that, as he seemed to really like his ride, *but* he simply set it back up and then we talked some more.

Eventually, however, there wasn't as much talking as the brief kisses became more intent. He was drawing me close, leaning me back, and kissing me until I could hardly catch my breath. My head was spinning as he caught me up close—it felt perfect. But then I noticed we had slid ALL the way down in the seat and his hands were sliding. *No. No!* In spite of how I felt, I began sitting back up, and I guess I must have said it out loud, because he leaned back just enough to ask, "What's wrong?"

I know my eyes were probably as big as saucers and my voice was small, because all my emotions were spinning out of control. But in the back of my mind, I could hear Mrs. Dean and Mr. White, my Sunday School teachers, reminding me what girls do and what godly girls do. I didn't go into detail on that, but since I'd asked him and he'd *said* he went to the Baptist Church, I assumed he would *know.* I was hopeful that, despite the rumors about him, he was going to understand and take this next thing well.

Quietly I responded, "I don't do that."

His questioning response, "Ever?'"

My honest answer came, "No, never."

There was a moment of silence as he looked at me in the dimly lit back seat. It was a long enough pause I thought I might be needing those shoes back on my feet to get me home. (I seemed to be forever trying to figure out how I was going to get home these days!) But then he began kissing me again. Gently, softly, deeply. Then when I was drifting away from common sense again. He stopped.

"It's almost over. We better start getting you home." And with that, he climbed into the front seat, and I followed and off we took.

I gazed over at him as we hit Race Street attempting to read his mind or expression, but when he caught me smiling, he simply leaned over and kissed me reflectively. Settling atop the console, his arm around my waist, we cruised through Searcy and headed 13 miles west toward my home. I was glad he had been paying attention, because I had missed the double part to that double-feature, and this Cinderella's clock was about to strike midnight. As it stood, we were just going to make it. Six hours had felt like minutes.

Inside I could feel something alive and stirring within me as a sweet yearning filled my head and heart. It was so different from anything I had ever known or dared dreamed of. So unexpected. So quick. My mind tried to say it was all too quick, but my heart outpaced it. I didn't know it showed on my face until I walked into the house twenty minutes later and caught my reflection in the mirror. Stopping, I leaned in. My eyes were alight. My cheeks flushed. A smile lay half-ready on lips that had just kissed his goodnight. That's what it looked like then, this thing called love.

৩০৫

I woke up the next morning after another dream, but this one wasn't scary like some horror script. I was married to Lenny and we had two kids! Now, I'm not silly. I knewwww it was just a dream, because I was the girl who wanted a WHOLE bunch of kids. That was part of the plan, so being married to him with JUST two kids *had to be* a sleep dream.

I walked through the morning with my head in the clouds, humming while I got ready for church. Mom and us kids went every Sunday mornings, although we always arrived at the last minute because we kids were watching TV. Dad worked or stayed home but very rarely went with us to church. Anyways we went to Sunday School. We sang wonderful songs. I heard a beautiful message. And then, after church, my wonderful morning was doused with a reality check, as I caught slack from my friends for being back out with Lenny.

Everybody always seemed to know everything about my private life. I had not *even* seen a soul I knew at that movie. But someone saw me, I guess, and now the world knew where I was ten to twelve hours ago. But what if they were right? Maybe they were. They had known him far longer than me. What if they really were right? It got me wondering, he might NOT show back up at the Fitness Center Monday, and while I tried to act unconcerned, I did have to face the fact, to understand, that this could be the outcome.

But when Monday night rolled around, so did he, right after his shift at work. Looking good! For someone who didn't like pretty boys, I sure was a mess. And he always smelled great!

I was just glad to see him, and when he walked up and kissed me on the lips for all to see, I figured we must be all right! I was also a bit embarrassed maybe, but I was relieved more than anything. The joy I found just having him near was indescribable. It made my heart sing. It made everything appear black and white, and only the two of us had color! It was beautiful, and I was loving every second of it.

After he finished his karate class and a Nautilus session, he hung out with my sister and brother as I finished up with a client. Then I walked with him outside as he prepared to head home. It was super chilly, and so when he said, "Jump in for a minute," I did. We talked for a little bit about where he had worked and was working, making small talk, but eventually we would get back to "stuff" that seemed more relevant and definitely more fun. In the stillness that followed, I leaned back against my car door so I could face him. He looked sexy (sorry, Mom). I felt … happy.

And then just out of the blue with a dreamy lilt still in my voice I asked a simple question. "Lenny, do you think we'll ever get married?" You might be saying now, "*What*! You did not ask that!!' Yupppp I did.

I didn't think it was improper. It was what I was thinking, so I said it.

His look was priceless, in a way that wasn't entirely positive, and that's when I realized that this probably *wasn't* a good question for someone you had dated once and only known eight days! So I quickly tried to clarify and back out of the odd situation.

"Well … I just had a dream. We were married … and had two kids. (Why can't I shut up!) But don't worry. I know it's not true because I am going to have nine."

That was supposed to make it better. At least before I said it, it had sounded like a "you-are-off-the-hook" response. However, that's not what I saw or felt as he quickly said, "I have got to go." Then reached across my lap, opening the car door, giving it a push and then me encouragement to exit ASAP!

I stood there stunned as he pulled out without a wave or a kiss and watched his taillights disappear.

Dazed I re-entered work slightly stunned. Welllllll, that might have done what my dad and uncles couldn't. I knew it was possible—and, according to the consensus, probable—that he might not be back around for sure now. Walking into the Nautilus Center, I busied myself with work resolving to be content with the outcome. I was trying to sound mature and grown-up, but my head and heart were all muddled. Finishing up, I prayed in waves of confusion to a God who thankfully was and is never confused even when having to sort through His daughter's unfiltered messes.

6

Lenny showed back up the next night as if nothing had happened, even winking at me as he headed back to change into his karate gi. Just like before, he practiced taekwondo and then did the Nautilus routine before going to hang out with my siblings and some other youth in the front lounge. Hmm, maybe we were okay? It looked promising.

My lil' sister had just vacated the seat on the couch by him when I entered, so I settled in beside him listening to the ongoing conversation. I don't know what they were talking about and didn't try to catch up on their discussion. I simply sat afraid to speak, since that last episode had left me thinking I needed to *shut up*. Then he reached over and grabbed my hand up in his. Exhale. *Whew, it's okay. Beautiful. Now I can relax and we'll just pretend nothing ever happened. I'm cool with that …*

Suddenly Angela, my black-belt ten-year-old sister, came bounding back into the room scolding me for taking her seat. We all just chuckled, and she quickly redirected herself into the loveseat across from us. Next thing I know he was talking and she was interrupting, asking to see his class ring. (Great Scott! Is it a genetic thing? Does my WHOLE family talks out of turn?) Absently he let go of my hand, laying it on his leg, and removed his ring and gave it to her. Reaching across for my other hand, he immediately continued his conversation about cars and parts. I don't know much about them. Wait! That's not true. I don't know *anything* about cars, so I simply enjoyed how closely he had drawn me in and being able to rest up against him.

Catching her fumbling his class ring, I turned my gaze to Angela, ensuring she was being careful. She was just slowly examining the pictures on the sides and occasionally bursting out with those endless questions, so I turned my attention back to Lenny, which was much more enjoyable. Finally satisfied, she stood up and walked back toward Lenny and unclasped our hands. I don't know what he thought, but I thought she was putting it back on his finger INSTEAD she slid it onto mine!

Embarrassed, I stopped her and quietly and as quickly as possible said, "Angela Renee! You *cannot* do that!"

We were at a stand-off as she held my hand with the ring on it. Her matter-of-fact response was filled with correction as she said, "Well, you two like each other *and* kiss AND hold hands, so he should be your boyfriend." (That mouth thing is going to be the death of me. Somebody tell the Feltrop closest to you to SHUT-UP, please! I am dying here!)

This wasn't just the two of us in his car now. This was a *half-dozen* of us in the lounge with passersby filtering through. I was totally embarrassed and half-scared he'd be flinging gravel again if

I didn't do something. Quickly I redirected her attention and began to remove the ring, but then Lenny placed his hand back upon mine that bore the ring. I paused, confused, and looked up to find him gazing fully into my eyes as we had been *before* that "married with kids" comment was made.

His eyes were tender and wrapped me up in that feeling I cannot define. Then warmly he said, "I like it there. Let's leave it."

Once again, I was blushing—this time with a focused audience. I was grateful when a client came in so that I could physically escape the looks and smiles—well, almost grateful. :0)

He was still there when the advanced karate class was finishing and I started my close-up jobs. In fact, he was holding the door as I came down the hall on my way to the dumpster. Doesn't that sound romantic. Not so much, huh? But it is what you make of it. :o)

Following me outside, we crossed the front of the studio and turned into the alley to access the back of the building. There he took the bag from me and we made small talk, mostly about who was afraid of the dark. We didn't talk at all on the way back. With it tossed in, we only made it as far as the shadows on the side of the building before he grabbed my hand, encouraging me to stop, and leaned into me as I rested my back against the wall. Oh, how I'd loved to have stayed there forever, but we both knew as soon as that class was done inside and my sister was free, we were going to have company so reluctantly eventually we headed in.

Before he left he asked me out for New Year's Eve night. I, of course, said yes.

Driving home some time later, I actually didn't need or want to listen to the radio as my heart was dancing to a melody sweeter than anything I'd ever heard before. Maybe Mom, Frankie, and Angela were talking, but I was wonderfully lost.

ᏉᏉ

Friday night he showed up looking good and smelling great, two things I would learn were to be a constant with Lenny. Since he had picked me up at Aunt Mary and Uncle Kenneth's for our first date, this was his first time actually in my home. Frankie and Angela were both watching for him to pull in and ushered him inside, where we sat and visited with my folks before we took off towards town a little after eight. Mom had asked me what we doing earlier, and I had told her I didn't know. And that was the truth. When he arrived, she didn't ask him. Neither did I. But I did get an extended curfew to 12:30. This Cinderella just had to be headed home by the time the sirens stopped.

The streets were actually quiet, but we did a couple of laps, cruising up and down Race Street. It was a bit early, and it was so cold outside I figured all the others were meeting at someone's house. It didn't matter to me. I was happy with some small talk and his hand resting on my thigh. It appeared as if he knew *everybody*, as there was constant honking and waving (at him or by him), and with each one he would tell me who they were and where they were from. I thought it was remarkable that he knew everybody by their car, but the truly amazing thing for me was that he could tell me who a person was by simply seeing their headlights coming down Race Street! But what did I know? We had so little traffic on Morris School Road that I guess I just hadn't developed all the right skills. LOL

ANYWAYSSSS, we cruised. From the Van Atkins parking lot, down to the Sonic, and around the Court Square and back. I remember stopping only once, and not for long, as nobody's heater could keep up with the damp chill that hung in the air. The only way cruising is an effective interactive event between different vehicles of people is when you can either get out to enjoy a visit *or* roll down your window. Tonight, it was *way* to chilly for either of those options. Quite frankly, I was gloriously content just to be at his side.

But eventually we pulled into the Piggly Wiggly parking lot, and after an hour we made another loop and stopped in the Hancock's Fabric side of the same parking lot. We talked some and kissed some and watched cars go by, until restlessly he put the car in reverse and backed away from the street, all the way back to the front of the closed store, into the shadows so we could create our own heat. From where we now sat, we couldn't have identified a car if we had wanted to, as our windows were quickly fogged over. However, a half an hour later we did recognize someone was pulling up as their headlights created a crazy, cozy glow in Lenny's Camaro. Reluctantly we sat back and he Lenny rolled his window down once again to visit as I sat blushing warmly on my side of the car trying not to looked "kissed."

Leaning back in my seat, I listened contentedly, and when the car took off, I knew two things more. One: he understood I didn't party, as he'd just turned down a New Year's Eve party invite. Two: he wanted to be with me more than his friends. There was something so precious and timeless about those moments that followed. He held me and loved me, without asking me to compromise anything. Strangely enough, while I wasn't the one in the driver's seat, I spent the next few hours having to remind myself where the brakes were.

Eventually the sirens broke our beautiful interlude. We pulled back and leaned into the silence, holding hands as we listened to cars honking New Year's greetings to other cruisers and waiting for the defroster to kick in. I decided to help out just a bit on my side, lazily reaching up to write across my moisture ridden window … Lenny 'n' Sherry.

And we headed home.

The year 1982 had ended on a beautiful note.

Welcome 1983.

જ⚬ન્

As wonderfully as 1983 had started off for Lenny and me, it wasn't so great for me when I got back to school as it all just flared back up again. Who didn't know about the nineteenth. Gordy and the "Camaro guy"? They knew about Lenny. They knew about him coming to the studio. They knew about New Year's Eve. Of course, I was wearing his ring, so that added fuel to an ongoing fire with the very peers at school who had *just* started cutting me slack for breaking up with Gordy a month before. And Gordy, well, he still wasn't talking either, so I didn't know how much of what they even said about him was true. For all I knew, he was getting as much unwanted counsel and grief as I was! It felt as if I was walking through one of my nightmares, except instead of *not* being able to change anything, I seemed to have this innate ability to make things worse and everybody mad. And that was not me, although I seemed to be acing it at this moment. It wasn't my track record or personality. But just as I couldn't break free of the crazy dreams at night, I couldn't stop whatever this was going on *in* and around me.

By the time I got to work Monday afternoon, I was mentally and emotionally undone, and just grateful to be away from my school peers and all the input. When Lenny showed up, I immediately felt relief. So much talk had gone down AGAIN about who he was and what kind of man he was with the ladies that I had begun to question our relationship and anticipate our end. It loomed almost bigger than anything we had shared, because it was reinforced by so many guys I called friends, not just those who were buddies with Gordy but simply boys I'd grown up with who were concerned for me. Actually, they didn't have a problem with Lenny as their friend; they just were all aware of his way of dancing to and through women and didn't think he should be my friend.

Well, duh? Isn't that why I sat between him and Debbie? Geez! What was I doing? We weren't just dating and steady. I was giving my heart away. Too late for me. I was all in already. The dye was cast. Thankfully, tonight wasn't going to be the night he decided to bail, so I didn't have to worry about it now. He was here tonight.

And you know what?

I believe everybody can change. So there was hope, *but* I also
knew I was going to need to hold steady and use more caution. We
had pressed the limits on too many boundaries on our two dates.
And as much as I loved to be with him alone, I needed a better plan.
It was one thing to fight off public opinion. It was another thing
to ward him off. But this battle wasn't with him or his past. This
battle was within me. As everything in me longed to be consumed
by him, but my faith, the Voice in the night and my mind, said
to resist my feelings and my flesh and maintain integrity. I am so
thankful for all the years God spoke to and directed me on those
hills. That relationship sustained me in the midst of this all. That
Voice reminded me that this was a battle I could not afford to lose.

7

In my childhood, the enemy was visible.

A malicious, mangy pack of wolves circled the boundaries of my home. Want for hunger had brought them to our door for within its walls they smelt life. My brother and sister were hidden in the back closets by my mother as she tried to keep them hushed and out of sight. The windows offered little protection as the predators threatened to attack the thin glass veil every time they saw movement.

Silence prevailed except for the occasional sounds of weeping as my little sister quaked and cried and my brother clutched onto our mother, trying to be brave.

*I was moving ever so quietly around the house, desperate to find
a means of escape so I could go for help. I headed to the kitchen,
hoping to get to the carport and the car and listened carefully at
the door. All the howls and snaps seemed to have moved to the
back of the house, so I slowly eased open the oak door. Seeing
nothing, I began to plot my next step. Yet as I swung the door
wide enough for me to exit, a low growl erupted in the fading
light of day and suddenly a half-dozen wolves moved in slowly,
with drags of saliva falling from their panting mouths.*

*Closing the door ever so softly, I leaned back against the wooden
frame. How long would they stay? It had been hours since I saw them
running toward our home from across the newly mowed field on the
other side of the road and raced inside the house to warn Mom.*

*Now all light had faded from the sky. Outside all that could be
heard was the rare snap or snarl and the sound of their paws as they
paced about the walls of our home. Still at the door, I sat unsure of
what to do, and then I heard it : Dad's car pulling in the graveled
drive. Quickly I rose and looked through the window only to see
him gathering his keys and coat, preparing to come into the house.
Without thought I raced back to the door, watching as the dome light
came on and he pushed the door open. I could see them then—black
shadows crawling toward him. I couldn't move. I couldn't speak.*

I awoke, my chest aflutter, my breath in rugged gasps. With eyes
open, I once again prayed my way through one of the dreams that
would return again and again throughout my childhood and youth.

Recurring dreams happened throughout my early years. Always
negative or dark. Always threatening those I loved. Crazy dreams
for anybody but *especially* for me—a girl who lived in a safe little
cocoon with *no* scary movies *and* who lived for the type of singing
and happiness found in Disney's *Sunday Night at the Movies.*

Scary stuff? Hmm … I was just a country girl who lived with her beautiful but imperfect family in a rural area of the foothills. We were just simple country folks who loved to be outside separately together. We had only recently gotten over our excitement about having a party line phone in our area. (That's an old-fashioned wall phone that had different rings because three or four families shared the same line. Google it if you have more questions or better yet ask somebody over sixty ☺)

We knew our neighbors, even though the closest ones were a half-mile away. AND we trick-or-treated at *all* their homes. People weren't scary. Different, yes. Scary, no.

I would have said I had many friends, but I had no *close* confidants.

I would have said I was good with people, but I found my sweetest times were alone and away from the crowds.

I dreamed when I was awake and when I slept and would say with full confidence that I dreamed in color and could awake with total recall. But I was informed those are both wrong, and maybe that's just as well if the dreams you have are as overwhelmingly real as my nightmares were.

Right now, I don't know what to think. I guess my life is filled with discrepancies.

I do know whenever chaos slid into my thoughts, my nightmares would return to haunt my reality.

ৎু৵

*A lofty, moss-laden cliff with an incredible view of the horizon
beckoned families to leave their cars on the side of the road
and cross the short expanse of woods to its edge. Parents strolled
arm-in-arm, carrying picnic baskets and blankets. Children
skipped and raced ahead. All were in their Sunday best, and
all were halted by a barbed fence spread at the woods' edge that*

stretched as far as the eye could see. Scattered along its entire length were large precautionary signs: Do not cross. Danger.

One impatient young boy ducked under the strand and raced, laughing toward the stretch of green grass that lay like a carpet between the fence and the cliffs edge. Quickly his dad hurried to retrieve him, but when he saw it was safe and saw nothing that caused him alarm, he turned and beckoned his wife and daughter to join them. Slowly but surely, all the families threw caution to the wind and eased onto the sun-drenched lawn, spreading their blankets so they could stretch out, eat, and play with the world spread at their feet. I was there too with my family, in a bright yellow pageantry dress with bells tied up in the many layers of my skirt. My dark hair was held back with a matching bow.

It was a beautiful day to be with family, yet I was uncomfortable as I crossed the fence and the warning signs. As others played—I sat on guard. Distracted by the beauty of the moment and the breathtaking view, buried under the sound of singing and laughter, they all failed to see or hear it slither and scratch its way up and over the side of the cliff. I sat immobilize. Hearing it. Watching as an old, gnarled, deathly gray hand crept over to where a child idly played near the cliff's edge. It's thin, hairy arm seemed to have no end as it just kept coming and then stilled. For a moment it was almost indiscernible, but then, in a blink, it moved snatching the child up, quickly descending back over the elevated ridge even as the youth's limbs struggled trying to break free.

I raced to the cliff's edge, ignoring my fear of heights, and lay down prone on my belly in order to see its descent. We were soooo high that the clouds were far, far below us, and I lost track of the arm as it drew down below the mist. Still straining to catch a glimpse I saw instead a now empty hand returning, ascending once again. Immediately I begin calling out to the multitude of people around me, "Get back behind the fence. Everybody move back beyond the fence!" But nobody listened. And then I saw it as it grabbed a young girl with golden locks. Her mouth opened as if to scream, but neither her voice nor my own could break through the joyful chaos the others were enjoying.

Finally, at my family's side, I breathlessly explained what I had seen, visibly shaken. With tears cascading down my now grass-stained dress, I pleaded, "Please listen. Let's go!" Yet even as I pleaded, pointing to the edge where I had last seen it, even as I began attempting to pull them to their feet, I saw it arise again. It was coming again! My voice was gone. My eyes were huge with disbelief and red from tears. I bowed my head. I could watch no more.

I awoke breathless, scared beyond reason, for although I knew it was a dream, I could feel evil trying to wrap around me. This dream came so frequently I began waking up my little sister to talk and play games until the fear had subsided enough for me to try to pray and attempt to go back to sleep. In the weeks since I had begun dating Lenny, they had been recurring frequently. Prayed up and prayed out, I decided the best place for our dates might be my house, where boundaries might remain more in tack. I could barely handle the nightmares that came in the dead of night, when I had no voice or escape. I could not risk having one infiltrate my day. I just couldn't …

৵৵

We had an open campus at our school, and since school had started back, Lenny had begun picking me up during lunch. We far too quickly got out of hand in that thirty minutes, so as the week headed toward another Friday, I prepared to share my idea regarding future dates. But when we started talking about the weekend, I found we had a different problem than what I imagined. Apparently, my school was having a dance, and he had assumed I would go and take him.

Problem. Here was another thing I didn't do. I didn't go to the dances. It seemed our relationship was forever doomed with roadblocks, where we would need to figure out how his ideas and mine were going to merge. However, I did understand how heavily our differences could weigh on something so new and fragile, so without much ado I tossed it all to the wind. It seemed I was forever creating or giving our love another opportunity to fail.

In that moment I suggested he go ahead and go to the dance—without me.

He looked stunned for a minute, then questioning, as if maybe I was trying to make a joke, or maybe it was some sort of test. I just sat. Loving him quietly. At peace with what must eventually come. Maybe it was a test. We both deserved the right to know where his affections lay. He had always said one of his passions was dancing, so if that was something that was integrated into his heart, then we both needed to see how that would play out for these two opposites. It was a statement. A suggestion. He leaned back, gauging my eyes, puzzled.

Then he said, "You'd trust me? You know, of course, when I dance I will be dancing with another girl? You are okay with that?"

And I said without anger and with all the unspoken love I felt but could not voice, "If I can't trust you then you aren't mine already. Soooo I guess we should be finding it out." I didn't say it sarcastically or in mean spirits. I wasn't judging, hating, or even afraid. It *really* was more important to me that he be happy than I be his.

Suddenly suspicious, he asked, "Well what are *you* going to do if I go to the dance?"

That was sweet. It appeared he might be jealous. I smiled and gave my best guess. "I'll probably ride around with Melissa or Pennie after work—then go home."

And that's how that Friday night was planned out. Four weeks in and we were going to have another test. My friends were concerned for me. My family was quiet. I was strangely content.

Above all the chatter that continuously revolved around his character, I knew that sooner would be better than later if he was going to break my heart. I was already too far in, and though he hadn't asked for it, my heart was not beating its own rhythm anymore. Before I lost myself completely, I needed to know where his heart lay, and if I was the only one fighting to keep from whispering in the stillness of our times together, "I love you."

I went to work Friday afternoon, slightly preoccupied but calm. A little after nine, after finishing work, I jumped into mom's car with my official new driver's license in hand and went off in search of Pennie or Melissa. I pulled in and talked to some of my friends who were also not dancers that were hanging out behind Van Atkins off Main Street. Then, with no sign of Melissa, and finding Pennie on a date, I decided to make one loop down to Sonic and then back to the courthouse and before heading on home.

As I headed back toward the court square, I heard a honk and turned surprised to see Lenny in the realty building parking lot, next to Poor Boys Burgers. I whipped into Poor Boys having been going too fast to turn in where he was. He met me as I stepped out of the car with a kiss. I don't think we ever had a simple kiss—*each one* seemed to leave me beautifully undone!

Then curiously I asked since I didn't actually know anything about school dances, "I expected you to be at the dance. Didn't it last until midnight?"

He smoothly responded, "I went, but I didn't want to be there with someone else. I wanted to be with you." (Wow! that should be in a storyline somewhere Oooohhhh it is ... it's in mine LOL) Then we began doing what we loved best. Leaning against my white Volkswagon Rabbit, my arms around his neck, his hands at my waist ...

Suddenly I heard a girl's raised voice and we both straightened up. I didn't know what was going on, but she was angry—at me. My eyes were wide in disbelief. I was totally clueless, and somehow I missed the whole first part of her sentence, but *no worries*, as she was still making her thoughts known as she came in closer. One thing I did know—I had never seen her before, so whatever was going on had to be something to do with Lenny, not me.

Lenny had stepped between us as she started repeating herself, attempting to get in my face. He tried to stop her, speaking calmly and even affectionately, "Dindy ..." But she cut him off, intent upon informing me of how the cow gives milk (that just means she was emptying her thoughts on a matter, and that matter was *me*!).

"I don't know who you are, but this," she said, pointing toward Lenny and slurring slightly, "is my brother, and ... and ... and I don't know WHOOOOO you are ..." Once again Lenny tried to interrupt, but it wasn't happening.

Her long blond hair was moving with each turn of her head. Her slurred words were unwilling to be silenced "This is my brother, and I DON'T know who YOU are, but he HAS a girlfriend already and I am fixing to kick your *!#*!." This she said as she attempted to sidestep Lenny.

This time he not only stepped in between us but physically took hold of her arms. The loss of momentum seemed to silence her, as he finished what he had initially tried to say. "Dindy. *This is* my girlfriend, Sherry. Sherry, this is my sister, Dindy."

She started laughing—actually, her laugh is an inside chuckle you can hear. I kinda liked it. Then she apologized, saying that she just wanted to make sure nobody was hitting on her brother when he was already taken. Then, leaning in closer, she whispered, "Sorry. I normally don't drink, but I had some punch tonight and am a lil' drunk. Want some?"

She smiled. I smiled gently too, refusing.

A moment or two later we were gone in Lenny's car. That night back in between Hancock's and Piggly Wiggly he would whisper that he loved me. I don't know which was sweeter, hearing him say it to me or being free to say what I had known since our first date, "Lenny, I love you." We actually talked a lot that night about heavier things in life and about protective boundaries for us. Before we separated we agreed our dates on the weekends needed to be at my house, as neither one of us seemed to trust ourselves anymore. He would be over Sunday after church.

8

That first Sunday went fine. In the country, you find ways to amuse yourself. Lenny had learned that by experience the first time he picked me up for a date. That day, my brother had come out with us as we were getting ready to leave, wanting to show him our idea of fun. (Warning: Here comes the redneck in us. I'd like you to believe that it's too corny and therefore *has* to be made up, but the truth is this was one of our recreational activities. LOL)

Okay so there was a huge old oak that grew behind the kitchen window. Under that oak, and off to the right, was our huge butane tank. Above that tank extended one tired oak limb, worn bare and smooth. What we did was hop up on the tank and lunge for the limb. The trick wasn't the jump, as the top of the tank was less than four feet off the ground; the trick was hanging on as the limb kept springing back up even as your weight made it keep bending down. I guess it was kind of like a primitive bungee cord—that makes it sound almost legit, so let's roll with that :o)

Frankie had jumped up eager to show Lenny how it worked. He had great success. I skipped it, not wanting to look foolish, but Lenny decided to try it. Rather than jump up on the lower side of the tank however (as it was on an incline), he opted to jump up on the high side, like a cowboy, running and doing a jump and straddling over the hind quarters of a horse! He was actually successful in the jump up; *however*, his pants didn't make the stretch and ripped out from the front to the back. In the eighties we wore our jean T I G H T. Luckily, he just "happened" to have an extra pair in his Camaro, so as soon as he had grabbed the limb and bounced down, he went in and changed, and then off we went.

So, with that start to the entertainment at the Feltrops', it could only get better.

Okay, Mom did pull out home videos one day, and even I was bored to tears, but Lenny never complained. The rest of the time we shot guns and did target practice. We rode three-wheelers. If he was there on a Sunday, we went out with Dad and my siblings to cut, load, and stack wood. And we took walks, long walks, up into the woods alone. Those were my favorite.

By the time our second full weekend was swinging around, my mother let me know that I needed to start pitching in to feed my fella, and so I became responsible for soda, ice cream, and snacks when he came over on Saturdays and Sundays. So now I'd get my check from Mr. Brown. Fill the car. Get the groceries and go back to broke *again.* However, it was easier to spend time together without the fear of going too far. I just had to watch those walks in the woods, because I really did like his lips on mine. Being held in his arms. His body pressed against mine. Doesn't sound very godly, huh? Yeah, that's why we came to my house. And that's why we didn't stay as long as we would have liked to in the woods. Initially it had been to keep him from pushing, but then it was school lunchtime visits in the Camaro and nights at the studio taking out the trash and Friday nights after work. I'd come to realize it wasn't about trusting him. The truth was I trusted him in those moments more than I trusted myself.

When the car died on us at lunch two weeks later, we were parked up above the school on a hill. Lenny ended up having to walk and find help and bring somebody back with jumper cables. That was embarrassing for me, because I "knew" the older gentleman "knew" exactly what this seventeen-year-old girl and twenty-year-old boy were doing on the hill in the chill of late January. It felt like God, my preacher, and my dad were all there with us when he raised his eyebrow at us and said our being there probably wasn't a good idea; nor was it any way for him to treat a lady. *Ouch*!

Could it get worse? Yes, because by the time we got the jump, I was late for my next class. While we could leave campus for lunch, returning late was a very, VERY big deal, creating a twofold problem. Lenny knew one consequence: I would not be able to leave the campus for one to three days, but more than that I hated getting in trouble, and I really liked our vice-principal. But that wasn't as big a deal for me as the other situation. The class I would be entering late would be my DECA class, and EVERY day it seemed our discussion centered on Lenny, me, and my relationship with Gordy. If I came in this late, the boys weren't just going to be discussing my stuff; they were going to be *fussing* at me, and I was going to turn a dozen shades of red while they discussed where I'd been and what I'd been doing, and Mrs. Mosley wouldn't be able to save me until they were done. *Dadgum*!

We sat in the car while I tried to get the courage to face it all. I just didn't have the guts to face my class. Lenny, sensing my problem, suggested we just go kill a few hours and then he'd bring me back at the end of the school day. That worked for me. I didn't have a problem skipping school, just with getting in trouble for being late. So off we went towards McRae. When we got to his folks' house, he went and borrowed his neighbor's three-wheeler, and we went riding. Then we went in to his house to clean up as I had to get back to school on time and be at work immediately after.

His sister and parents were at work. And we ended up in the bedroom. You know it starts off wrong but easy and then gets to feeling right, but it is wrong. It feels unnatural to love somebody so much yet have soooo many brakes. We were just kissing. Just kissing. Have I mentioned how much I loved being kissed by him? Then we were moving on and doing what we did in the car and in the woods, and then everything accelerated … Whoa!

I interrupted it all suddenly, sitting up, speaking barely above a whisper, totally breathless. "I have to stop. I can't." My Cinderella ending came with some things unseen and untouched until you were married. In my mind, those came with a ring—and *not* a class ring. Intoxicated, but not with drink, we backed up. He showered. I questioned *everything*.

Rolling back toward town twenty minutes later, we clasped each other's hands as if we weren't letting go but said almost nothing. Once again, when I wasn't sure what to expect, he surprised me as he stopped next to my car in the school parking lot and caught my chin gently up so that I was forced to make eye contact with him. "I love you. We're okay." And then he kissed me gently and let me go.

Weeks went by and talk settled down completely at school. Gordy had a new girlfriend. And I guess everybody had given up on reasoning me into or out of anything. Lenny and I were fine, but since the trip to his house, he seemed to approach the "danger zone" way quicker. I understood it was hard but loved God too much to settle and Lenny too much to let him go. Even though he was the first guy I'd ever really dated that hadn't talked about wanting to marry me, he was the first guy I couldn't picture living without. But that was where our relationship sat. It was time to take a step forward or let it go. We were back to the commitment thing that I had been warned about since I first met him.

Then the last Friday night in January he altered our "norm," saying he needed to run out to his house to get something. I was a little guarded, but he also seemed a little quiet. And as he was the only person I wanted to see this evening, off we went in his car. I was grateful to find his mother was home, and he introduced us and then took off to get whatever it was he had forgot. As quickly as that, we were off again, but he was in a stormy mood. I'd never seen him like this before. I didn't like it, but as he didn't respond when I looked at him questioningly, I let it go.

He looked intense, and even when he touched me there was weight to it. It was different. I had thought we were going to hang out at his house and *then* go downtown until it was time for me to meet my brother at the Junior High Gym, but EVERYTHING about Lenny was so drastically different that I was glad to be heading back early. I didn't understand what was going on, but the heaviness was so physically present I was ready to call it a night. He had something going on and didn't seem to want to say it, and so let's close the book on today and wait for tomorrow. We'd be good.

It *was* all good. It had been for six weeks. I told him I loved him. He loved me. We whispered it almost nightly. I didn't doubt he meant. I believed him. I believed my words as well. I knew what I felt. In my heart. In my head. In the Lord's ears when I spoke of it to Him at night. Somewhere along the way, all my fears had been cast aside. I had begun living in a dream that I never wanted to end. Every day built up into something sweeter than the day before. Every touch had new meaning. Every day was a blessing. I didn't speak of marriage. I didn't feel a need to do anything but reach for the day as it unwound.

My lunch schedule was a rendezvous, with him tasting like the Poor Boys burger he consumed before he picked me up and me tasting like some fruit-flavored Mary Kay lip gloss. (That made for a great combo there! :o) His trips to the house were safe and fun, not as provoking as we both might have liked but definitely safer. My family loved him being around each weekend, especially Frankie and Angela. We had an unplanned pattern that we were rolling in. Life was beautiful. Love was sweet.

But on this night, everything seemed so different. And when Lenny halted the drive to Searcy suddenly, saying he wanted to show me where he went rabbit hunting, I thought he might be wanting to talk about whatever was going on, and I said nothing as he slowly turned the car onto an overgrown road into somebody's woods halfway between McRae and Searcy. We reached a clearing of sorts. He turned off the car and turned to me. Rabbits were not what was on his mind. It was dark now, so I couldn't have seen a rabbit anyway, and I wasn't shocked when I felt his hands reach out for me and pull me over. But it felt different. He drew me in (normal) and over into his lap (normal), and after an extended session of heated close contact (normal), he had me slide back onto the console. I understood why he was uncomfortable, as we'd been in this situation before, but I was expecting the same response as before, which was to shift gears and cool it down, but tonight wasn't going to be like those other times; instead, he spoke of things I struggled to comprehend, and then he held me unwilling to walk away empty-handed tonight.

I felt my heart stop even as my eyes tried to seek out his in the dark. But he said nothing more, just retained my hands as I leaned away from him in what now seemed like a very small space. The more I backed away, the more determined he became, and then I started silently crying.

He loosed me suddenly then, sitting back in his seat. Mad. Then he started in on me. He was talking, but I was thinking.

This might be the end, because I wasn't going there and he wasn't backing down.

Reaching into the dark behind me, I grabbed the door handle

and slung it open. Stumbling out of the car, I started walking across the field blindly. His words had cut and were cruel. *No* love. No devotion.

I was broken. Not afraid of him but resolved.

Weeping and completely unable to gather my thoughts, I was a hundred feet out in the field when he called my name and asked me to stop. I stopped. I didn't understand what was going down. Then I also realized I had no idea where I actually was or which way would get me to Searcy.

So I stopped. In my tracks. Standing there as he toned down his irritation and told me to come back and get in the car so he could give me a ride to the truck. If I would have known where I was I'd have walked, but since I didn't, I quietly complied and slid wordlessly into the passenger seat but nowhere close to the console. He stiffly offered an apology, and then it began as he started turning the car around and heading back to the road: the "I'm sorry—I need time" speech. I had heard that before from camp boys, and it had wounded me. This time it was coming from a man who I was in love with, who I had tasted heady waters of passion with. A man that made me laugh and my heart sing just because he was nearby. If it had been day, I would have noticed the sun being ripped from my world. But in darkness the void just seemed to swallow us up, as it had the landscape around us. I said nothing and tried to halt my tears, as they seemed to make him more agitated. Eventually we were on the highway, and he had no more words in the air begging for consideration. I'd never found anything to say.

As he hit the gas, I shot a glance over at him, but his face was fixed like flint, straight ahead. Before we reached town, he repeated it. At least this time he sounded upset and tired rather than so angry, and it sounded as if it had a question in it, but my mind did not have any question.

To ease him, I said what my mind was telling my heart. "It's fine.

I understand." He glanced up and over at me but I couldn't hide my hurt or my affection and tears, and slowly he looked away.

"Sherry," he said softly with his gaze fixed ahead on the road, "I've told a lot of girls that, but none ever responded like you just did." There was no movement on his part. He didn't try to reach out and hold or comfort me. And I couldn't catch enough light to read his expression. All I could hear was the regret in his voice, but no apology followed.

Slowly I cupped my hand over the other that wore his ring as the tears continued unchecked down my cheeks. Slowly spinning the ring that had said to our world that "I was his" my mind resolved itself in regards to what I must do next. He wouldn't have to ask me for it, but I was struggling to take it off. I left it on until he pulled up by the truck. Then I turned toward him, reaching across the dark, and handed him the ring.

Would he have spoken? I don't know. I just knew I needed to. So I pressed on tearless and spent, softly stating *my* reality. Simply and without condemnation. "I'm not mad. I love you. I *want* you to be happy."

It came so calmly I didn't even recognize my own voice because the tenderness denied the fact that my heart felt as if it was being crushed. But with that said, I lifted my head and looked him in the eye for a brief moment. He started to speak but then stopped and looked back straight ahead. I slid out of the car and began walking toward the truck even as my brother was advancing towards Lenny's car. My family loved him too.

Having seen my face in the parking lot lights, however, Frankie stopped. Then I heard Lenny take off. It was done. Frankie followed me back to the truck, wise enough at fifteen not to ask questions or say anything. And even though legally I was supposed to be the one driving, I couldn't stop my head and heart from flat-lining, so I had my lil' brother drive me home as I starred blindly out of another passenger window.

9

Nobody at school was shocked that he had dumped me; they were still in awe about how long we had lasted. Thankfully, they did not all feel the need to restate their opinions about my judgment. It being what it was, they probably knew almost as quickly as I had about our breakup. They were all actually very nurturing those first few days back at school, much as my family had been. Sure, people tried to pry and find out what had happened, but my business was just that, *my* business. My friends and family knew I kinda held my cards tight to my chest. The truth was I also still loved him. I didn't want others to go back to thinking less of him, so I tried to just eat the glances and probing questions when they came. My family didn't know much about him anyway, so they were easier to be with. My friends and peers at school and several from work did *know* him, and since I wasn't getting mad, they were.

I was handling it well until he showed up at the karate studio a week later. I actually hadn't expected him to come back there. After all, that studio and those karate classes were run by and filled with my friends and family, and while they didn't know the details about what went down, they *knew* I was hurting and he was the cause.

But I was glad I had taken the paycheck, that I hadn't had to spend feeding him the previous weekend and bought me a cute blouse. Initially my thought had been we would make up prior to Valentine's Day and I would have something cute to wear. Today I had given up and wore it hoping it would cheer me up or at least give the appearance that I was doing better so everyone could ease up worrying about me. Actually, they worried *for* me. I don't think they questioned my strength, because there was an iron in me that God had planted in my childhood. I rarely, if ever, found it necessary to voice my deepest hurts, even though my countenance might give me away. But today I found myself struggling to hold back tears and smile. Today I found myself wishing ... wishing I could lie.

The shirt was meant to be my decoy. It was white with a light pink bow at the collar. I knew it looked good with my auburn hair and coloring, as it made my cheeks seemed flushed, pink, and pretty. I also hoped it made me look ... carefree. Overcoming. On the mend. I just didn't like the sympathetic glances. Tonight, I was also intentionally NOT thinking about it being Friday night. So I was focusing on encouraging the clients swinging in to work out. They were keeping me busy. Most were old friends and most were older than me, so it was easy to keep the conversation on the workout *or* the day-to-day things going on in *their* lives. It was going good— *until* Lenny marched in.

As soon as I possibly could, I slid to the back to the women's dressing room, deciding it was a good time to hang back and check the whirlpool temps and chemical levels. It wasn't my normal time, but Lenny had been visiting folks and lingering in the foyer. I knew he was baiting me. I knew he had seen me. I had caught him watching me. His face once again set. My face flushed, struggling to keep back any show of emotions. I wasn't ready. I still fell asleep each night spent by tears in prayer. I just wasn't ready.

I piddled back there long enough to listen to two Hall and Oates songs. I had stalled as long as I could in the back and, knowing his karate class should have started, I edged out into the hall. He was there waiting and advanced to meet me. Stiffly I said hello, taking in the fact that his hair was as always flawless, recognizing immediately the stirring scent of his cologne.

I also recognized the man I had met two months before was back. Soooo full of himself. Arrogant. This wasn't the man I knew. The man I loved. I looked him in the eyes and then in the face, unwilling to let him see my vulnerability. That's when I noticed them—hickeys on his neck, all over his neck. They actually gave me the courage to speak when all I wanted to do was run away.

Matter-of-factly, I verbally acknowledged their presence. I guess I hoped it would make him uncomfortable and he would continue on his way to the men's dressing room and let me pass.

But no, that wasn't going to happen. Without remorse, he leaned in and responded, "I've got plenty more in places you'll never see."

I stood speechless and no longer needed the blouse to make my face appear blushed.

Then he passed me by as I sought strength not to let it show. I was barely able to stand. I felt physically sick and was utterly speechless. But my mind was spinning, and one *very* wounded/ frustrated thought raced across it—all I had to do was share what happened. All I had to do was say *one* word to *any* of the instructors or my upper-level students, and when *he* came to class they would mess him up just a tad! One word …

But as deep as he had cut me, as betrayed as I felt, I saw him in the next moment much as I saw my father: weak, selfish, and adrift without the ability to reign over his own life, *completely* unaware of how his choices were affecting those who cared for him.

Resisting tears once again, I walked back to the front desk and busied myself, ignoring the questioning glances from my peers and coworkers until I had gathered myself together. Everybody knew we were at odds. They all knew I was struggling, and I was thankful for theirs and Mr. Brown's grace in that moment. Finally, I saw him go into class, and I headed back into the workout arena.

Our clients, my friends, had graciously been waiting on themselves. Now I was back to work.

ᔤᔥ

He left immediately following his class without a word. I watched and prayed and waited for the clock to get to nine. I was emotionally and mentally done and in need of some solitary time to loose the floodgates I had been holding in.

What I wanted was what I couldn't have.

What I needed was to be held by someone who knew my pain and its depth without me saying a word.

I went straight home and to bed. Betrayed … overwhelmed … undone.

Lying in my bed, I found more tears flowing from my eyes from some endless resource I couldn't restrain. Not wanting any attention from my sister with whom I shared a room, I slipped out the sliding back door. The coldness of the winter night grabbed at me as I slid once again onto the swing, starring up over the hill behind the house to the skies until I felt the One who calls Himself my Friend—the One who is the Lover of my soul—wrap Himself around me. His peace rested upon me in that moment, and in the days to come He alone would be my confidant.

It didn't take Lenny too long before he had a new steady. I didn't go around asking or looking for information on him. People just assumed I would want to know. The things he had once said we would do, he did for another, and as she was a classmate, I fought daily not to look up for him at lunch as he came to pick up another girl for his adventures.

He left in good company.

I sat alone but not lonely on the front steps of the auditorium, fighting memories of our lunch dates only a month before. They were torturous ...

So went my days, days followed by nights begging God for help.

In the weeks that followed, I endured his presence on our campus, endured others girls being with him, but the hardest thing to fight was my heart. I didn't want to give him up, and in the late hours of the day, as I lay and prayed, I found another voice following my Amen. It weaved horrible realities of what had been. It stole my innocence and made my love for him dirty. It whispered that I was wrong and he had never cared. My feelings were the lie. It pulled at me as I wept until my tears were exhausted and I begged God for mercy. Mercy for him ... but more urgently, mercy for me. My whole world was growing dim.

I had never felt so numb, so dead. At school, at work, and with my family, I'd just throw up the face everyone wanted to see, but the nights became consumed by a strange new voice offering me lies and drawing me toward the darkness, until one night I found myself at home alone, contemplating death, a knife in my hand and the weight of loss shutting out every particle of hope I had ever clung to. Around me were the things of his I hadn't returned—the note from the roses he had gotten me after we met and other little notes he had left me lying around at work. His picture.

Tonight I was a mess.

Earlier this evening I had been standing at the welcome booth at work when he came in to the studio sporting the shirt we had discussed making but he had laughingly stated he would never wear. But he had one on today; however, it didn't showcase our names, as I had hoped to see a month ago. It was his with his new steady's name on it.

Neither of us said a word. I stood still, too physically exhausted to turn away. He went straight into Mr. Brown's office. Though he had entered with his gi in his hand, he stayed just long enough to meet with Mr. Brown and make eye contact with me. Then he turned and left.

While he was in the office my heart had raced on! I needed to stop this. I needed some type of closure so I could move on. Reaching into my purse, I grabbed the five-by-seven enlarged picture I had had made of the wallet pic he had given me. While we had dated it had sat on the stand by my bed. Afterwards, when I was trying to convince everybody I had moved on, I had removed it from there and into my bag, as I was my own worst enemy and carried it around trying to remember who he *had been with me* rather than who he was again.

It was time to try another avenue to letting go, so with it in my hand, I headed out to where he was preparing to get in his car. He was moving fast tonight, so I said his name hoping to slow him up.

"Lenny?" My voice was fragile as I was unsure he would even bother to stop for me.

He stopped halfway in his car and stepped back out toward me. I needed to speak quickly before I lost my nerve and momentum.

"You'll be needing this." My voice didn't bear much weight or confidence as my emotions were stirring but I wasn't crying just crossing bridges. Then I handed him the picture.

His gaze went from hard and set to slightly hurt, and when he responded he sounded puzzled. "I don't need it. You can keep it." Did he remember it had sat by my bed? Did he remember I looked at it every morning as I welcomed the day and every night as I told him goodnight and said my prayers for me—and for him?

I couldn't do this anymore. Determined to be done I responded, "Then give it to Nancy because I don't need it either."

It sounded brave, except since I can't hide my feelings from my eyes and our eyes were locked, I knew he could see my heart there. Quickly I turned away, not knowing what I was supposed to do with the question I saw in his own eyes as they had searched mine.

And now, hours later, here I sat alone at home. The card from my roses, the little notes he had given, the original wallet picture I kept in my Bible, and a knife lay beside me. Except for a sliver of light that came from the hallway through my partially closed door, it was dark. I sought strength but kept finding only pain as my imagination raced over our past and slashed wildly at what I had felt so strongly about. Despair staggered my heart with hopelessness. The tears had stopped an hour ago … I was ready for the pain to go away.

Yet, even now, I couldn't help but want to protect him from more scrutiny, so, slowly and with great effort, I gathered everything up and went outside to the burn barrel. I could barely move. My body felt so heavy. Every step was a lifeless effort. My mind was giving up. My body was tired. My heart had bled out. I couldn't feel a thing anymore. The darkness beckoned me as I dropped the notes and picture in one piece at a time. Then I had to pull up enough energy to strike a match, and as I did, anger struck me. It wasn't about protecting him; it was about being free from the pain of him, and even as I sought a final purge and lit one of the notes, I stopped seeing the fire catch and reached down, burning my hand, unwilling to let the flames have his picture and my memories.

In rushed the pain where the fire had bit at my hand, and in came a fresh onslaught of tears as I clutched his image. With my emotions re-engaged, I realized where I was and what I had been contemplating. Steadfastly I moved further away from the house and the burn barrel into the rim of the wood line in front of the barn. There, falling to my knees, I bypassed the taunts of the one who had held me poised moments before, and then I collapsed on the ground, pleading for help. Alone. Broken. Brokenhearted.

I remember wanting to ask questions as I started to pray, but questions would not come. Instead, in their place, came a prayer I had not prepared or ever heard or spoken. Shocked, I heard it as if it came from the voice of another; yet it was my lips moving in petition.

"God, if I can help Lenny be all you would have for him to be, bring him back to me. But if not … if not, help me get over him."

Then I lay doubled over until the tears would come no more.

Much later, as I rose, I collected the knife from the side of the now cold barrel. Re-entering the still dark house, I took it back to the kitchen and then put his picture back in my Bible and fell asleep spent.

It was done.

10

The darkness was a weight. It held me bound. Locked up. Where was my Help? I believed in miracles. I believed in the God who was capable of delivering them, yet in the prevailing cloak of nightfall I felt my prayers for Lenny's return slammed down repeatedly as I pleaded with fervor like never before. The air was heavy. My thoughts consumed me once again as my eyes frantically searched thru the darkness looking for him. Where was he? Lenny? My insides were knotted in despair. Twisted. My heart lay in my stomach, a knotted, sinking thing, drowning. Lost. Was the whole world oblivious to my terror! I wanted to scream out for help but had no voice. I wanted to continue to pray but didn't like the answer that kept overriding my broken pleas. I was falling into a darkness that

*seemed to have no end. The hands I had clenched in prayer were
grasped so tightly that pain started to shoot up my arms, but the pain
piercing my soul was overriding everything else. My world swirled
upside down and became a blur in the night. Then, silence …*

ৎ৵ক৶

Nightmares wore me out during the night as much as my own pain
wore me out during those days. Often in the stillness of nightfall
I could hear the one who hated me pacing outside the house. I
was in a battle for my sanity. I prayed often. But when no one was
looking and I dropped my defenses, all looked dim and my heart was
exhausted, torn. My mind was visited by the foe that had whispered
death into my stillness. As surely as I fought to move forward, my
world inside was in chaos. Prayer and retreats into the hills were
my solace as this new enemy continually tried to convince me I was
alone and what I had thought I held was as much a figment of my
imagination as the dreams that blessed or haunted me each night.

But time heals if you allow it to, and that's what I needed.

But you must have time.

It seemed before I could get it together he always managed to
step back in and unravel it all again.

Another month had gone by. His actions were … well, I just
didn't know the guy I kept seeing downtown. My heart would lunge
when my eyes spied him, but my stomach just knotted up in denial.
That guy in the Camaro didn't look at all like the man I knew.

I had let some water flow under the bridge. Talked with some
fellows, including the pastor's grandson. I had been on some guarded
dates. But everything felt wrong. So I opted to skip romance and
just hang out and embrace life. I was two months from graduating
and the world was fixing to unfold before me, or at least that's what
I wanted to believe.

When our rural country church had an event for the youth and children in mid-March, renting the whole roller rink, I was down for some fun with friends. It wasn't because I had any talent on the floor, because I definitely did *not*. Debbie was pretty good. Truth was that in order for me to feel truly accomplished I needed to be skating with some little kid who couldn't stand up and struggled to grasp the concept, because that's me on skates. Ugh!

Oh well my church family was my extended family and we saw each other more than I saw most of my blood kin, so what did it matter if I was slow or occasionally on my butt! As we circled the rink that night, I realized how good it felt to laugh at myself again. I was in love with the music, which flashed me back to earlier days, when I had gotten my first eight-track player (I hope you young folks have unlimited data because you may have to Google that too in fact while you are at it spend some time enjoying our awesome music!), and I was singing with the Bay City Rollers' "Saturday Night" and KC and the Sunshine Band's "That's the Way I Like It." It was more than good—it was a beautiful relief.

Looking up, I spied Robert sliding in and hollered for him to get on the floor, laughing as I rolled on by, lost in the music. My brother seemed to only have a fast-forward speed, so I was on guard, watching out for him and his friends because they only knew how to fly forward. They didn't know how to stop, and that was a problem for everyone else. My sister wasn't going as fast; she just never got off the floor. Just watching them was making me tired. Debbie was there, swinging in and out, but much like school, we were great friends but not comrades.

Frankie came, brushing past me *again, totally* ignoring all my warnings and the signs that said *No Racing*. Not a minute or so later I felt someone snag my hand as they raced by. I looked up assuming it was Frankie or Robert, but to my surprise it was Lenny, who *didn't* go to our church. I watched him circle by my sister, and she was so excited to see him, as was my brother. Dang! He even skated well, crossing his legs to make his turns, and the next thing I knew, he passed me, going backwards, and gave me wink. Aw, shoot! I felt myself blushing, and I should have been mad. I should have been cautious, but I just smiled back, and then they called for couple's skate, and there he was, before I can get to the edge and slide off, taking my hand.

"Come on. Let's go." And I did, as if nothing ever happened. Frankly, in those moments, it felt as if nothing ever had. I wasn't angry when he kissed me while we were alone on the dark end of the rink as "Endless Love" echoed across the almost empty floor. I was graciously abandoned as we circled the floor. But then, just as suddenly as it had begun, it ended, and the lights came up as an all-skate call went out. And he was gone.

A few days passed, but no word came. I was confused, but neither Robert, Debbie, nor my family said his name. Saturday, I went running around with Pennie. I was actually going to spend the night with her and just meet my family at church. In reality, I was hoping for a distraction but found none, as Pennie, who was also on the rebound had started dating Jay, I was left hanging with whatever safe friends showed up downtown. When she finally did show back up, we headed to her house (because I had a curfew regardless of where I was). I was ready to go to sleep. But what I encountered next robbed me of that thought, as we entered her home to find the entire place thick with smoke. As I passed through the room, I was offered liquor and weed. As tired as I was, I knew I could not stay there and told her so when we got to her room. She said she didn't want to stay there either, so I ended up calling home, not just saying we were at her house but asking if I could just bring her home with me. Mom, of course, said yes without questions, and off we took.

It wasn't until the next morning we realized that Pennie hadn't brought church clothes (which I don't think you can Google, but remember it was *always* dresses, hoses, and heels). Mom graciously allowed us to head back into town to get her clothes, as long as we promised to be back for preaching church. But on the way to town,

I had a thought, and as my thoughts had been on Lenny since the rink, I decided to move on it before I got all tangled up again between what I perceived and what he was thinking. Stopping at a gas station, I called him at his home.

I was moving too fast to be working off of any plan. I was winging it. His mom answered the phone and off I went.

"Is Lenny there?"

"Yes," she replied coolly.

"Could I talk with him?"

"Hold on and I'll get him for you."

Then there was a moment of silence before I got his groggy "Hello?"

"Lenny, I just don't understand," I said, rushing in before I lost my nerve. "I don't know if you cared *or* care for me or not. But if you do, could you slide up and meet me at the library? If not, it's fine. That'll tell me what I need to know. But I have to be gone by 10:30 for church."

He said he would be there just to give him a minute, so I dropped Pennie at her house to shower and change and drove six blocks over to wait.

He didn't show.

At 10:30, fighting tears and that taunting voice that always plagued me these days, I left rubber to show where I had been. I headed out to pick up Pennie and took off quick in order to get us to church on time. If I'd have waited ten minutes there might have been another ending to my day, because I'd have seen him slide in looking for my truck or car, but I wasn't there. Learning something years later didn't change what we both felt in that hour. I took his failure to show up on time as a *no*. And he didn't bother trying to follow up with me.

ട─ര

After that I started shooting from the hip. I was totally burnt out and overwhelmed, unwilling to go back to that dark place *or* to wait. I guess something just snapped. All I knew was that I didn't want to slide back into that vicious cycle between prayers and despair again. Soooo I dated. I went out with Harold and with Charlie. I talked with some guys from the karate studio. Gordy had a girlfriend, so I didn't look that way. It did feel good not to be un-chaperoned when Lenny saw me in town. It felt nice to see *him* stop and stare because I was wearing somebody's letter jacket. But the whole thing left me feeling wayyyy wrong, and I didn't like them touching me. I tried, but every date left me feeling hollow.

So I started trying to make sure I had some connection with a fella before we went out.

Ricky and David had been friends of mine since Junior High, when we'd been in choir together. They were also Lenny's friends, but we'd started hanging out back when Ricky was dating Pennie. I enjoyed the boys. I was comfortable with them. I always felt like they had my back, especially Ricky, as he took on a kind of big-brother role. And when he asked me out, I said yes. I wasn't worried about Lenny, because he was *forever* moving on, and I didn't think for a second about Pennie, as she was dating someone else and seemed to have moved on away from Ricky.

We went out that night on a double-date with Bud (one of my friends off the school bus) and his girlfriend. Now here we all were at the movies, and we tried to make it feel right and romantic because we really did see and appreciate the best things in each other, but it just didn't. He said it, but I knew it as well. I did continue to hang out sometimes with him or David. I didn't quit thinking they were great catches, just not great catches for me.

Drama was everywhere! The prom was coming up. A date? I had gotten to the point where I didn't trust myself to make sound judgments. I was a confused mess and wondering how my life was going to be any different when I graduated next month if I couldn't tackle this heart thing. Shoot! I couldn't even walk through the silly prom thing.

In the end, I opted to gather a bunch of my girlfriends. We would go together and skip getting dates. So five of us chipped in for a hotel on the other side of town so we didn't have to worry about our curfews. We lied to our parents about where we were staying (I just didn't have it going on, Mom—sorry) and got dressed up. Oddly, none of us had ever really attended a regular school dance, yet here we were, dolled up for a formal one. (Oops, that's another lie, as I had attended one, because I felt safe knowing I had friends going to be there, but Lenny was also there and so my exit was swift.)

We girls enjoyed the meal and getting our picture taken, but by the time the dance was in full swing, we were already gone. They may have stayed if I had, but I figured if there was a dance, Lenny was sure to show up and I just couldn't do it. So off we slid to McDonald's to fill up on real food instead of that frou-frou stuff they had served us an hour before. Then we went to the hotel and changed back into our real clothes and decided to go out cruising for a bit.

Stopping by Dandy Don's for my bottle of Coke, I was taking a sip as I looked up and saw Lenny spot me and honk. Dang! We could have stayed at the dance after all, because that joker was out and about on Race Street. Exasperated, for whatever reason, I went to plop down in the driver's seat without dropping the Coke bottle down and hit the steering wheel with the bottle, which hit and chipped my tooth! I was SOOOOOO DONE with bouncing in and out whenever I saw him. I couldn't do this anymore.

It always took me a day or more to get past just seeing him. I *had* to stop, but how? That night as I lay in bed, it came to me. I had friends in a new territory where Lenny was *not*.

It was time to get out of Searcy.

11

My mom, brother, and sister opened a karate and aerobic studio in Heber Springs (more than thirty miles north, by the lake) that spring. Several of the guys that had been driving to Searcy for karate classes lived there, including Scott and Doug, so I just headed that way every time Mom and them did and I could. It was good. There were friendly faces and new faces. A new environment. It was good to not be on guard. I still wasn't dating anybody, but I also wasn't even looking to date. I had set all the heart stuff aside and was enjoying being able just to be and breathe, which I hadn't seemed to do well when I was having run-ins with Lenny.

As graduation eased in I was prepped and ready for something new, but I and my dad were on different pages. I had found a college at Crowley's Ridge that I was interested in attending, but my preference was a girls-only college in Kentucky. I knew I was shooting for space from Lenny, but my dad was a hole in my road about as wide and deep as the Grand Canyon, and he wasn't buying or paying for either of those. I wasn't going to have a scholarship, like my cousins, because I had slept or read through the memo that my high school grades would have any effect on financial awards. Or maybe they had those meetings on one of the days I skipped out. Truth be told, I was lucky Mr. Mallet liked me enough to call me to the office and inform me that all my absences would result in my failing if I missed even *one* more day. It appears I had skipped out twenty-nine times. (Please, young family members, don't use my name as an icon on how to finish your senior year strong! I'll tell you I was stupid and come kick your butt all the way back to class!) ANYWAYSSSSS all my older cousins had gone off to school after graduating OR went in the military OR ended up staying at home. Yeah, I *needed* to go *away* from Searcy, so something had to happen.

But just as my world was opening up, here he came again. Not at Searcy. Nor at my work, where I had just given notice. Not at some school function or in front of Dandy Don's or Piggly Wiggly, but at Heber! How did he even find out *my* stuff! He doesn't even live in Searcy, and I totally quit hanging out there! But there I was, talking with Scott and some of the guys, and there he came down the hallway not five minutes after they headed into class. Once again, I was immediately flustered. I was half-angry. I was half-afraid. Dang! I could always act indifferent when people talked about him. I just couldn't pull it off when he was around!

With no place to hide and no one else around, there was nothing to do but make small talk. He watched them working out, and I focused on the clock on the opposite wall, praying I could harness my feelings for the next forty-five minutes. And I was amazed as the time seemed to fly by, and in no time they were dismissing class. Hallelujah! It was time for us to track back home!

Yeah for me! I wasn't crying. I hadn't shared too much. Of course this time he also hadn't even touched my hand or arm AND I hadn't looked directly at him so I couldn't catch 'the look'- which is probably why I still had my wits about me. Regardless of why, I was good.

However, tonight, *everyone* seemed to be moving so slowly, and we couldn't lock up until everybody was done and gone. Scott small talked with Lenny, and then my sister came over and they were joking around. I knew they missed him, but they needed to S T O P! But instead, oh no, they aren't thinking about my feelings *at all* as my brother walked up and *invited* him to go grab a bite with us.

No way! You have *got* to be kidding me—was this my life? Really?

Yuppp! It was because *my* family has no clue what had transpired over the past five to six months; *nor* did they *know* what kind of man he really is, because they'd have never done that to me if I had told them anything. But I had told them nothing. I had hidden everything. So there we were on our way to the Sonic. My brother, his friend, my sister, mom, me, *and* Lenny. Go figure.

Lenny invited me and my siblings to ride with him but I was driving my new old Maverick that I had brought Frankie and Angela up in after school, so I had a good excuse (rather than a rude one) to give him for not accepting his offer. But my siblings and their friend jumped in with him to drive over.

When we arrived, everybody just sat in their cars. I ordered my supper, and Mom was ordering theirs. I didn't know what Lenny was doing, until he slid out of his car and went over to talk to my mom. *Wonderful! Everybody's bonding!* I was sooooo angry, and sarcasm was dripping off of EVERY thought that crossed my mind. I just wanted my burger and to go home. But then here he came—lucky me!

Wasn't his hair ever just jacked up! I had to fight my stinking curls and frizz *every* day, and yet, there he was, looking good and smelling good and flooding my senses with things I didn't want to remember! I didn't want to talk to him alone. Everything was coming undone, and I was so afraid and frozen.

My window was down already from placing my order, and as he strolled over, I began preparing myself. Ready for a touch and another one of his quick takeoffs. But I wasn't prepared for what came next.

"I talked to your mom," he said, and I knew he was watching my eyes because I was watching his as he continued, "and I have permission to ask you to come up and spend the day with me here at the lake tomorrow." I glanced over to where she was in her car, but she was talking to Angela and avoiding me, I think. I felt betrayed. I turned back to him, kind of difficult not to do when he is leaning in on your window, and waited. But he was too close, and I had a hundred feelings trying to fight for first place as he continued. "Your mom said if I didn't really care about you, I should leave you alone. I told her I loved you."

My green eyes were locked on his hazel ones as unshed tears and fears filled my eyes. I knew what I felt, but it seemed as if I had been here before, and this never ended well for me. My mind was racing, considering a dozen different thoughts, feelings, and ends. Surely, I reasoned, we must be at a different season now, and we could do this. Before the thought could even complete itself, I heard my mind say, "Run!" and simultaneously screaming in the distance, my heart said to seize time with him, and my flesh cried out for him.

Suddenly I found a safe compromise. Looking at him, I said, "I'll come if it's okay if I bring my brother and the boy spending the night with him tonight."

He said that would be fine and he would see me at the bluff site swimming and camping area in the morning. Walking back over to his car, he paid for his food then drove away.

So here I go again …

ஒ௸

I won't lie—I went to bed excited and woke up with my heart wide open. He had been in and out of a half-dozen relationships in the past three months with none lasting more than a few weeks before he dumped them or they caught him cheating on them. *Yet* he had intentionally and consistently made an appearance in my world every two to three weeks since we had broken up. Maybe this was it. Maybe he wasn't lying. He had said it again without prompting. Without me saying it back. He loved me still.

But in spite of my hopes, I warned Frankie not to wander off to far from us, not because I worried about my brother but because I was worried about me. We met him at the lake but waited for him to shower before we headed to town so we could grab a bite to eat. Talk was on the light side, as it must be when you have a fourteen- and a fifteen-year-old boy with you. Then we were back at the lake, and the boys were off and running, and we had space and we talked. He talked actually. He talked about loving me. He talked about missing me. And I listened. I didn't pay any attention to where my brother and his friend were. We were kissing, and then in the water, touching, and I dropped every wall. All morning. All afternoon. I emptied my heart.

Then, about four that afternoon, he started acting odd again. I had *not* said anything to set him off this time. I didn't know where it came from. One minute we were sharing a chip as my brother was snapping our photo. (Not my idea, his.) And the next he was saying he had to go. He had forgotten an appointment, yadda, yadda. So I told Frankie we were heading home and we loaded in the car. I didn't want him to be late for anything, and Searcy was an hour away.

But I soon realized I had a problem. My car wouldn't start. The starter was less than dependable but had been doing fine the past couple of weeks. But not now. And *my* car had *his* Camaro blocked in. I just said matter-of-factly, "We'll have to find someone to jump me or I'll have to call home."

He responded, "You'll have to, because I need to go."

That set my brother up fast and he told him simply, "You are not leaving us here stranded." He might as well have said "You WON'T leave us here stranded." My third-degree black-belt brother was one of the gentlest young men I had ever known, *but* he might not be someone you'd want to make mad—just saying—so Lenny got us help. Once we were started up, and as soon as I backed out of the way, he pulled around us and was gone.

It was weird. The whole thing ... weird. I hadn't asked for his pledge of affection. I hadn't been seeking his attention. I just assumed that whatever it was must have been important, and since I was a private person, I hadn't expected him to tell me his business.

But Monday, when I told Melissa we had been out and how randomly it had ended, she laughed under her breath, not a nice laugh, and squinted her eyes, making sure she had my attention.

"Do you *want* to know where Lenny went because I can tell you?" she said pausing momentarily as she watched my face. "Robert and I saw him at the movies with some girls Saturday."

I was deflated. "First show?" I asked.

"Yes."

Hating to ask but needing to know, I threw the question out there: "Flirty or friendly?"

She just gave me the look without a response. It was all that was needed. She and Pennie had walked just enough of this road the past six months to have caught on to more than I cared for them to know. They didn't even know the details yet Melissa hated him. Pennie didn't respect him. Disgust. Distrust. Animosity... they took on my hurt every time he passed by and left me broken. Yup, you could even call it hate. And here we were again.

How many times had I said I was done?

Well, it looks like I could add another.

I thought, if this is all about sex, then just say it so I can say NO and then you can leave me alone!

My head and heart were twisted, and I was tired.

12

Graduation was here. No more school! Melissa and I were off looking for the mandatory dress we had to wear under our gowns, although we would have preferred to roll up our jeans. We settled for two mini-dresses that were reverse opposites. Hers had a hot pink top with a turquoise bottom, so of course mine had a turquoise top with a hot pink bottom. (It sounds awful writing it now, but you might think the same thing about a mullet, cassette player, phones that remained stationary on a wall, and curfews. It was the eighties. Google our makeup and hair—it actually got worse as we singlehandedly knocked out a layer of the ozone with our hairspray!)

With much gratitude, a friend from the karate studio in Searcy fixed me up with a date from Beebe to chaperone me through my graduation. A blond, curly-haired Junior at Beebe High School, and a bit younger than me, Howell was super nice, and he didn't have a track record that required a data bank. Yeah, he was that nice. So all I had to do was make it through the lengthy speeches, and we, and Melissa, and Robert were in for a fun night. Parents and community sponsors had rented a theater, planned out games, and purchased door prizes; one of the local churches was even hosting our breakfast! We had a whole night of free fun before we all took off different directions. Now if I could have actually skipped the graduation ceremony, it would have been perfect! But that was not an option, as Mom would have none of it, which also meant we would have to stay around afterwards for pictures. But as Robert had to work at Western Sizzler that night, we would just meet him and Howell there when we were done.

We had a plan, and I was so looking forward to some lighthearted fun!

But the whole event dragged on and on, and the mosquitoes were *awful*, nipping at our legs. I was so jealous of the boys with their long pants. But eventually it was done. Hats in the air! Picture taken with friends and then with family. Now all that was left was to find Melissa. I stood on the field alone, the cap, gown, and diploma having headed home with Mom moments before. Where was she? There were still so many people, ughhh this was going to be impossible. Then I felt a touch on my shoulder and turned and got my joy button flipped off.

Here he was again, once again looking and smelling good. And all the love I felt for him tried to resurrect itself, but I was having NONE of it tonight. Not tonight.

"Congratulations!" he said and followed it with "Have you got plans for the night?"

I was glad I did, since I was such a poor liar. And I told him about them, maybe leaving out the part about just meeting Howell, but he didn't ask that now, did he?

Then Melissa walked up and grabbed my arm, giving him a go-to-the-devil look and led me away. I looked back once and he was watching us go. Sadly, I knew that if he had talked long, I would have been right back in it, whether it was for two months, one day, or a couple of hours.

So it was just as well I had friends watching my back. We met up with the boys and we did introductions as the four of us loaded up in Robert's car. Then we were heading back across town to the community center. We had just unloaded when Melissa said, "Everybody stop. I can't believe this guy! We are NOT going in there." I had no idea what she was talking about, so I followed her gaze toward the front door of the gym. There he was. The SAME GUY who had asked me less than thirty minutes ago if I *had plans* was heading in with another girl from my class to *my* senior class party.

I didn't know what to do anymore, and Howell had no idea what was going on as I looked helplessly at Melissa for help. I was just done. Done thinking. Done wishing. It was an endless fall with him. Every time I thought Lenny wanted to be with me, it just turned out he wanted to be with SOMEBODY and that's where he would end up. I couldn't go in there. I found myself weak, powerless, and hurting …

So Melissa switched it up and said we'd just go back and get Robert's car, and then they would find something to do and we could find something to do. The problem was they had been dating awhile and didn't have a problem finding something to do. We barely knew each other, but I was desperate to be held tonight and Howell was ready to do it. We were kissing in the parking lot when blue lights flashed through our fogged-up windows. I heard the cop talking to Robert and Melissa. Don't ask me why, as kissing isn't illegal, but I opted to take off like the good ol' boys from the *Dukes of Hazzard*. Sadly I hadn't been doing anything I could get in trouble for, *until* I pulled around the police car and left.

He was right behind me with blue lights a flashing when I pulled into the hospital parking lot to get whatever it was I had coming. What I heard, after he looked at both of our IDs, was that if I had been two days older and in that car with a minor I could have been in trouble. I didn't get a ticket, of course, but by the time we circled back to where Melissa and Robert had been, they were gone.

I asked Howell if he was done or not, and he said he had permission to stay out until morning. So we drove outside the city limits and sat on a hill overlooking Searcy. We talked a lot and actually found out about each other. He really was an incredible young man, and it would have been great if I could have felt something but kissing him only made me miss Lenny's kiss. But I sure was thankful for the hugs and affirmation he gave me. A little after midnight, I took him back to his car and said goodnight and headed home.

One thing I knew now beyond a shadow of a doubt was that I had to get *way* out of this town. I didn't want to wait for scholarships or fall college to start. I didn't want Dad to supply a car and spending money so I could attend the college at Beebe. Shoot! That was 8 miles or so from Lenny's house. How messed up would that make me!

Two days later, I had a plan. I would enlist and do college later and let the military benefits pay for it. With my mind made up, Sunday after church, as we walked down to go fishing in the Morris School Pond, I brought up the subject to Mom and Dad. Mom said, "What branch?" Well, that broke my train of thought, as I had not considered which branch, but Dad interrupted my need to think as he turned around and said, "*No*. And I don't want to hear anything else about it." And we all generally did whatever Dad said, so I didn't say anything else about it to him or my family.

At the karate studio in Heber, however, I did mention it to some of my peers as we loitered in the hallway, waiting for the advanced class to start. A couple of the guys smiled at me like, "You are kidding, right?"

But Scott spoke up, laughing under his breath, and told me, "Well, all I can say to the girl who won't take karate, because she doesn't like to sweat is don't join the Marines." At that moment, I decided I was tired of listening to *any* male for direction!

The next day, I parked my car outside the Marine Corps recruiting station. I filled out paperwork and was given a date to go test. Without telling a soul, in case it all fell through, I took the test and waited. When I returned to hear if I had made it in (because he couldn't call me at Mom and Dad's, of course), Gunny Vance told me I had gotten the highest score in the county in any branch, so I could pick my job and it was mine. All that was left was the physical swearing in and finding out when my job preference would have an open slot, as that would determine when I left for boot camp. Suddenly the only important thing was getting out of town. I said, "Can I skip the occupation preference? I just want out of here."

We talked for a bit about my dad's opinions on joining. I didn't tell him about Lenny. It hurt to think of leaving him, but that was the reason I felt I *had* to leave.

I told my parents that night I was going to join (but not that I'd already started the process), and Dad just repeated himself with some very stronger verbiage. I let it rest. I had already been given a date to go for the overnight physical and some other testing and swearing in, and I had a couple of days to plan, but there was one thing I knew for certain. I WAS going. And I WAS going to be a Marine.

I was trying to boost my confidence and intentionally stayed out of the way of my family members over the weekend. I told Melissa, but she didn't like it much more than my dad did. Then I stopped by to visit Ricky and David. They said nothing, but Ricky did raise an eyebrow, as if to say, "Are you sure?" And then he slipped off as someone pulled into the drive.

I visited with David a bit and washed up the dishes in their sink before I went outside to say goodbye. To my dismay, as I rounded the house where I had thought Ricky was, I ran smack dab into Lenny, who was with some really pretty girl (finally *not* from my school). I decided not to say goodbye to anyone and just kept walking toward my car, only turning as I prepared to enter it and make my getaway. That's when he hollered something about bringing him the jersey he had left at the studio, to which I replied, "Go get it yourself. I don't work there anymore." I slammed my door and took off.

The truth was his jersey wasn't at the studio anymore. Before I quit I took it home and placed it in my drawer so I wouldn't lose the scent of him. Pathetic! Stuff like *that* is why I had to leave. Why did I need his stupid shirt anyways! Dead set now, I made plans to run away. While everyone was at work, I loaded my books, stuffed animals (hey cut me some slack … I had had some of them around longer than I'd had my sister around), and clothes in the back of my car. Then, the night before I left to enlist, I snuck out, leaving a note. Knowing my dad might come looking, I didn't go to Deb's or Melissa's. Instead I went to Ricky and David's, where they hid my car and I laid low for the night.

13

The next day I caught a ride to Little Rock. I flew through the physical, paperwork, and additional testing and was waiting the next morning with a dozen others as we were sworn in. Done.

Now all I had to do was wait to leave, but when I called Melissa to pick me up, I got an earful, because she had gotten an earful from my folks. So instead of returning home, which I thought might be an option after I was sworn in and it was official, I called home to find out that I couldn't come home. Dad was that mad.

I guess I must have known he'd feel that way, and that's why I grabbed so much stuff before I left. But what I hadn't understood was how much that would devastate me. Home had always been my steady fallback from the world. Those hills were my private sanctuary. My family, my anchor that rooted me. I don't know why I didn't turn back to my faith—to God. I don't know if I was disappointed in Him or me.

God hadn't answered *that* prayer. Lenny hadn't come back to stay; *nor* had I gotten over him. I'd asked for one or the other. Either would have been an answer. But nothing had come of it. But then again, I hadn't resisted Lenny *and* I had started making my own plans *and* I had stopped praying regularly. Whatever the reason, I didn't call out to Him now; instead, I called my recruiter for help, as I was unwilling to put Melissa through anymore "stuff" on my behalf. He said he'd call me back in a few minutes. So I waited a little short on other options. When he did call back, he said his wife Becky said to come on over as long as I didn't mind a few boys hanging around and in my business. I didn't mind it. I was thankful, just glad to have a place to lay my head.

Going by Ricky's I picked up my car for one last errand. I needed to go back home and get the last of my stuff while everyone was gone. I was having a really rough week, and a word or hug from a friend would have been great; but instead, I pulled in to find Lenny there *again*!

There wasn't any small talk this time either; he just started back in on me.

"You can't go into the Marine Corps," he said in a manner that seemed to reflect that he, like my dad, thought he had ownership over this, *over me*! Yup, *this* was why I was going away. NOBODY needed two men who couldn't control themselves to attempt to control someone else, especially if that someone is me!

So I bowed up a bit and said, "I can and did." And walked to my car and took off.

When I got to the house, my face was stained and wet where tears had fallen as soon as I was where Lenny couldn't see me. Why did he have such power over me? Regardless of what I said or what it looked like, I loved him still.

I started crying again as I walked the hall and rooms, gathering the last little bit of my stuff. Those walls had seen so many of my tears fall over the past few months that they were not shocked to see them falling again as I wept for the family I could not see. The family I *had* had. The man I loved. The man I could not have. My life felt hollow—void.

I felt as if I had spent the last six months finding treasures worth celebrating, and *everybody* wanted to step on me and on them and crush the future my heart yearned for so desperately. All that whirled around within my heart, but inside I felt so numb. And you know what? I wasn't going to blame it on me. Not this time. I blamed it on the two men in my life, whom I loved above all others but who couldn't control their womanizing and liquor and life but expected me to follow their orders.

How do you go back and restart a life?

Was my life even worth the living?

I didn't know what to do, but I was ready to leave it all behind, and with my stuff in my hand, I started to head out.

I knew I was tired of feeling … so tired …

Then I stopped, hearing that unfamiliar voice that had plagued me the past few months. Slowly turning around away from the door, I walked back into the kitchen. Reaching up above the stove, behind the shortening, I found what I thought might get me through the day—my dad's crutch, a full pint of vodka. There had to be a reason he wouldn't just quit drinking. And if it did half of what every other country song claimed it did, then it should help.

I just wanted to forget. I wanted not to care. Not to feel.

Lenny was doing what he loved, dancing in and out of lives and beds, leaving me constantly devastated without *any* right to be, as we were *not* together anymore. He was gone.

And now I had no family. After all those times I had stood up for Dad when Mom was wanting to send out his cheating, drinking self, when I stood in the middle and busted up fights because he was out of line. All the nights I laid awake, unwilling to sleep until I knew he was home and all was good and our family was complete, and *now I am* out?

Is this what love really looked like?

Starting up the car, I opened up the bottle and drank. It burned, *but* I didn't care about the taste just solace for the ache. As I headed back into town, I just kept drinking and by the time I past Ricky and David's it was gone and the bottle was as empty as I felt. Then the tears came again, and I pulled over somewhere and wept. By the time I got to the Vance's, I was sick and hurting, but *at least this time I was* inflicting the wound on myself. I was tired of paying for everybody else's stuff. I was done, and not just with Lenny but with anybody who wanted more than a surface relationship.

When I got to Gunny's, I passed out on the couch almost immediately, until I got up to puke.

Then I shared my slurred state of affairs with Mrs. Becky, until I passed out again.

ৡৡ

I stayed drunk a couple of days. Drinking appeared to be what Marines did when they got together, so I fit right in. I found many of them were not unlike myself and were running from or toward something. But when I missed a Sunday of church, that didn't sit well with me. Even if God felt far away, even if I wasn't sure how to find Him apart from my church family, my hill, and some stillness, I did quit drinking but I wasn't in a good place spiritually or emotionally.

I was surrounded by guys, but these guys weren't my problem; in fact, they all took care of me. But I wasn't praying. I had almost always felt a close communion with God when we talked. When I prayed. But I couldn't even get a prayer started with the chaos within my head and the whirlwind that continuously repeated the last words of my dad and Lenny.

I had always had dad's back, so I really couldn't grasp what was happening. I knew I couldn't go to my church because Dad had asked if I was "going away to just stay away." Melissa and all my friends thought I'd flipped my gourd. And besides, I didn't want to make any more trouble for my friends. I did try to reach back out to Gordy, as he was planning on enlisting after school as well, but nothing brought me back to me.

One thing I *didn't do,* however, was go back to Race Street *or* to cruising *or* to David and Ricky's again. I couldn't take one more negative criticism.

It didn't matter if the Marines said I was golden, because God was as quiet as all the people I had loved.

ᔇᔕ

It seemed like forever, but in reality, I'd just been at Gunny and Becky's a couple of weeks, waiting for any opening that would send me on. I had drunk again, as I was out of cash and the boys offered me $25 to drink a can of beer. Okayyyy so they weren't taking care of me there, as they knew I'd quit drinking vodka, but because I said I'd *never* drink a beer, they were willing to pay to get me to do it, and they even bought me a 2 liter bottle of Coke to chase it down. I did it, but it tasted more *disgusting* than I had imagined! Maybe it was Mom's stories about it being made out of cow pee stirred with hobo rags, or maybe it was just because it stank! But when they offered $25 more for a second can, I did that too. Sadly, I had quit my job before graduation and had no money left and too much pride to borrow or call family members or friends. None of them—*zero*—were excited about what I was doing, and I didn't like people paying my way. My current situation, however, had made it such that someone else had to cover *all* my food and expenses. In my mind, I was justified because now I could offer help and pay my way. Two wrongs didn't make it right, but I did it.

I was still hanging out at Gunny's when I finally got a call, but it wasn't for boot camp. It was my mom, asking if I would be willing to go with my brother and sister to church camp, because they had said they weren't going without me. I was ecstatic. I was going to get to see most of my family *and* go back to Camp Wyldewood, where I could get my spiritual tank filled or me aligned. I needed something.

I was hungry for God, missing hugs, needing affirmation.

14

Two days later, right before I was to meet my brother and sister, I got another call. When Becky said it was for me, I cringed for just a moment, so afraid it would be a boot camp opening and I wouldn't get to go to church camp. But it wasn't. To my delight, it was an old church camp boyfriend—red-headed, barrel-chested Bob. He had called my house looking for me, and my brother had given him Becky's number. It's nice to have friendships (even if they were old flames) that always felt easy to step back into, and the Lord knew I needed somebody to have my back, to help remind me who I was, even if he did live in Mississippi. He had been hoping to come see me (which is crazy, seeing as we hadn't seen each other in two or three years), but it sounded nice, and then he started talking all crazy serious, saying that if I went through with the Marines, he'd sign up too and we could get married and travel together. Maybe *he* was drinking, or maybe he was just talking because that's what we teenagers tend to do when we are old enough to start looking forward but not old enough to actually do anything about it yet. We talked a long time, and just talking to someone who "knew" me was awesome! But I suggested he not go to the trouble of driving up, as I didn't know when I would be shipping out.

I had also been talking to Todd, one of the recruits who had just left for boot camp. I wrote him letters because (1) I thought he was kinda cute but, more importantly (2) they say in boot camp you *need* encouragement, so I wrote daily, as there was little else to do. He wrote back when he could. We were filling gaps in each other's lives. Todd was great, but the odds were we would not meet again, but I always enjoyed having someone to root for who would build me up in return.

When camp rolled around I was so excited to see my family. Even though we would each be in different age brackets, at least we would see each other.

Then there was Coach Grover: silver headed, balding, in his late sixties, *and* one of the godliest, most incredible men I had ever met. This would be my eighth year at Camp Wyldewood. The camp lasted ten nights and eleven days and had no electricity or hot water, but I loved it, and much of that had to do with the heart of the place: Coach. He knew *everybody's* name and was constantly hanging out wherever we were so he could see how we were doing and what we had been doing. He was the mood setter for the whole place! Beautiful!

Our actual counselors and cabin leaders were students from Harding College. This place was where I was constantly encouraged to read the Bible and never forget it was a love letter. Here they taught me to pray for my future and my future spouse. Here, friendships really did seem to bypass the time you weren't together so that when you were, it seemed as if you had never been apart. I felt like I was home.

The kids from the children's home in Oklahoma were there again, and over the years we'd gotten close. It was always exciting to see them unload, but every summer someone else wouldn't return, as they had left, grown up, or gotten a job and I lost a great opportunity to see an old friend. But whoever was there, whether they were from Oklahoma, Mississippi, or right down the road, we always had a sweet time.

I tended to make acquaintances pretty easily and always felt a necessity to create a "family" wherever I went. Inside I *still* didn't like discord or drama, although I had been living in it for a month. I just find it hard to stay mad at people who feel like family. And since sometimes there were differences coming into camp due to vastly different spiritual, financial, and emotionally challenged backgrounds, I jumped in with introductions, as this year our cabin leader was never around.

I loved the Spirit. I loved the energy. I loved being a part of it. I was grateful, even though the meeting with my mom had been a bit uncomfortable, just seeing her and her bringing me snacks like she always had. It was good. And after some time with friends and intentional time in the Word, it would get better. It always did.

Now there was nothing that had made me cut back in the Word because I had my Bible with me anytime I went away from home, although I had made that addition to it since last year. In case you forgot, I'll remind you I hadn't forgotten anything, and Lenny's wallet photo was still lying in its leather-bound shrine. Regardless of what I might say or imply to the contrary, my heart was still yoked to him. When I was angry or hurting, I would tell myself I kept it, because I needed to be reminded what kind of man I DIDN'T want. But the rest of the time it was simply there, reminding me I had prayed and to pray. Now that I was back at camp, that was easier.

I loved, loved, *loved* the music—all a cappella, echoing in the

stillness off the hills. I loved the passion of the men and women who
served from Harding. I enjoyed crafts but preferred to visit rather
than make something. And while I had never enjoyed the extended
hikes, they were good for me, because I *needed* to get my muscles
prepped for what was to come. I felt good inside and out.

One afternoon, however, something happened for which I was
unprepared, as Emma and Dinky from Oklahoma came in and
started asking questions, which is a *big* thing, as the two of them
were super quiet. But they asked questions, and I tried to answer
them to the best of my ability. Then I realized she was talking about
giving her heart to Jesus, and I grabbed her hand and led her out
of the cabin, intent upon finding our counselor or an adult, *but* I
couldn't find a grown-up anywhere! And when we had done a full
circle, ending up back at the cabin, I just jumped in, and we talked
about scripture and how Jesus knocked on our heart and gave us the
opportunity to say, "Yes." We talked about how it was a beautiful
choice but also a costly one, because Yes not only said you would take
a Savior but a Lord. It was a call to commit, to follow Him. I thought
I was just sharing, until a leader showed up to help us, but before
any adult got there, one prayed and then the other said, "Me too."

Wow! That was incredible! But I was scared I had left something
out, so once again we went to find a leader. It was incredible, seeing
as how I had just rededicated my life a couple of nights earlier, that
God had used me! I felt God reminding me that He was full of grace
and I was still … His. The favor I had felt for years but that had been
missing recently rested on me again.

Camp was flying by, and I was catching up some with my
siblings and friends and growing more and more excited for the
next leg of my journey. Then I had a visitor show up at camp our
last day. It was *not* Lenny or my dad or Bob but David, one of my
other camp boyfriends. He was from Oklahoma, and since our last
meeting he had grown and was taller than me. And apparently he
was a cowboy too, with boots and a bandana and a country boy's

worn cap. We talked for a moment about what he had been doing. He had actually been doing some rodeo events. Then I shared what I had done, enlisting, and in eight seconds or less he started talking about us getting hitched and him enlisting in the Corps as well. Out of the blue—no word in two years, and now here he is. What in the world was going on! I didn't look different. I wasn't posting flyers for a new flame (or an old one), but here was another one. And David was special.

We hung out that night at B-Rock and caught up, as it had been awhile since our camp romance. We held hands and kissed. He had actually been my first *real* kiss back when I was sixteen, and I jokingly told him as we walked down to the lighting of the cross that I liked it better when he kissed me now than I had then. It was nice, just to be with him. He had grown up. So had I. But the next morning, after praying about it, it just didn't feel right, and I asked him not to follow me either. I liked him too much to have him walk in anyone else's shadow. For someone who *needed someone*, I was sure wasting opportunities, but I still had Lenny in my head, and I was honest with David, as I had been with Bob. *Now* wasn't a good time for me to make heart choices.

We had just finished talking when Coach Grover flagged me to come to the office. I figured I was getting busted for that last kiss with David, but instead, he gave me a message.

GUNNY WILL BE HERE TO PICK YOU UP IN AN HOUR. THEY HAVE AN OPENING. PACK YOU STUFF.

YOU ARE IN.

I had already started packing as it was the final morning, so all I had to do was separate the things I would need to take with me to boot camp and get the rest to Mom. With that done, a sense of power welled up in me. I felt ready now rather than scared. My faith feet were back underneath me. And it felt good, like when you take a deep breath after you have been holding it *forever*.

It was time to move on.

I told David bye, and we cried as we parted (we always cried, as we were both kinda softies.) My mom showed up to pick up my brother, my sister, and my remaining items, and I cried then as well.

However, when Gunny pulled up in uniform, I was prouder still of my decision to head out. We loaded, and in no time we were on our way. Gunny stopped at Dandy Don's to fill up with gas as I raced in for sodas. With my sodas in hand, I turned around to go pay and then, *lo and behold,* once again Lenny was there. Every forward moving thought stopped, and so did I as my heart dropped once again and my mind turned to mush.

He asked what I was doing and I told him.

Then he *did it AGAIN!* Shot me down.

Then he starting fussing about needing his shirt back. So I informed him, "I am sorry, I just don't carry your stuff around with me. It's at Mom's. You know where they live, so *you* go get it."

Gunny came in to pay for the gas and then stood by the door. Lenny and I were having a standoff. Eyes flashed in anger and floods of other emotions swept back and forth in a silent war. When no one spoke, Gunny did. "Sherry, if you are done, let's go."

I didn't say anything else or look back. A stupid three-minute exchange had me locked up, and we were halfway to the bus before I quit trying to figure out why he bothered me so much. I decided just to let that image be a reminder of the man I didn't want in control of my heart.

15

Prior to boot camp, Gunny had been telling me to be prepared for mind games, but I was just half-listening, as eighteen-year-old youths tend to do. He tried to tell me again as we unloaded and checked my bag at the bus stop but my mind was elsewhere as I loaded up and pulled out of Searcy.

Around midnight, sixty of us girls were gathered up, from bus depots and airlines all over the United States, visiting and laughing and making new friends as if we were at a slumber party. *Then* I was wishing I had been paying more attention and had asked Gunny what exactly he had meant by that. Because when the Marines in uniform came busting through the doors, hollering at us and screaming out orders, I had no clue what I was actually supposed to do.

"Stand up. Shut up! Line up. Backs against the wall."

"Are you listening to me?"

"Quit looking at me, recruit!"

"Line up by your surname alphabetical order. No talking!" (WHAT? We don't even know each other's *first* names, and you expect us to line up by our *last* names? With NO talking?) *Phupf.* They sounded crazy, so I just opted to stand up, shut up, and put my back against the wall and then waited.

I had to force myself not to cry, because I never particularly liked being hollered at or fussed at. *My* personality says to do it right—the way it was asked—the FIRST time. *So,* being in this situation with no idea what they actually wanted me to do or at least how to fix it, I just fought to be strong instead of stupid.

Eventually they had us lined out. We sat through some orientation and walked FOREVERRRR. At three in the morning, we were finally able to drop into our bunks. *Exhausted*! Exhausted *and* knowing that the promised 6 a.m. wakeup call was not going to lead us into an easier day, because those people that had been *in our face* at midnight were going to be our drill instructors for the next eight weeks! Good thing I was prayed up before I got there, because I don't think I finished a sentence that night before I was out.

The next day was more instruction in loud, very loud condescending tones. I didn't realize "recruit" could sound like such a negative word! They took us to get measured, weighed, and outfitted with camis and boots, T-shirts and underwear. Then marched us back to where our suitcases were and told us to change into our camis and then line back up. Then we were told what we would not be taking with us: pictures, perfumes, brushes, combs, underwear. Then we were told, "You WILL be placing your civilian gear IN your suitcase, and THEN you will close them up and stand back against the wall. You will do so on my command. WHEN I say 'Quickly' … MOVE! When I say, 'Stop.' YOU ARE DONE RECRUIT. DO NOT SPEAK. DO YOU UNDERSTAND? (when were we suppose to actually ask questions if we had any??? Hmmmm …, good thing we didn't, as she didn't even take a breath before she said, 'QUICKLY! Annnnnnnnndddddd STOP.'

Then we were told that only two items were permitted to go in with us: prescription eyeglasses and our Bible. If we had either of those items in our belongings and we wanted to retrieve them, we would have five seconds to get them out.

"GO." I quickly reached down.

"1." and grabbed

"2." my Bible

"3." It looked like I was going to

"4." need it desperately.

"STOP."

I was done and standing at attention by STOP but still got yelled at. Anytime I moved, I did something wrong! And I'm not sure how long it took me to quit looking at them when they told me to quit something, because in *my* mind, if you told me to do something and then you told me to stop, I ASSUMED I was going to be given instruction on correcting whatever it was, so INEVITABLY I would look at whoever was doing the bossing. How do you fight off habits? Gosh, I was *stupid*!

Now, Sergeant Kerrigan would just squint her eyes at me and do a small shake of her head, *but* Sergeant Pollet, she *liked—no, loved*—to hear herself holler, probably because she was super good at it! But when I and the others realized that every time we didn't comply quickly, someone would be in our face, *or* the whole squad would be on the ground exercising or sent out to run, yeah, we are just going to do *whatever* they asked as quickly as possible.

Needless to say, boot camp was nothing like church camp, because I had to find *and* make time for reading my Bible, and *then* I caught a lot of slack for it. It wasn't that I didn't complete my other tasks. I *always* completed my tasks: a three-minute shower (including shaving your legs and underarms—now *that* takes some learning!), ironing my uniforms, polishing my brass and boots, straightening my locker, studies (because we had classes and tests just like high school). But when I got all of them done, I would read my Bible and write letters. They didn't say much about the writing, but they did comment on the reading, because they said I should be reading my manual, *but* I did that *during the day*, and regardless of my GPA in high school, I could remember anything I wanted to; I just hadn't wanted to then. I did now. Everybody always said I was sweet, but boy, it appears I sometimes took on quite *an attitude*. Bless my heart.

So I read my Bible anyway. Actually, I kept finishing in the top five with inspections, so they eased up some, except for Pollet—she just liked me I guess. Probably not.

I actually slept with my Bible under my pillow, largely because I didn't want someone going through my locker and finding it had Lenny's picture in it. If you remember, that was one of those things I wasn't supposed to have brought in. I could have surrendered it, but the honest truth was I would have had no way to get another, so I held on to it even if it meant I might get in trouble. Eventually, it didn't matter anyways, because we got far enough into the program that we could have friends and family send us small pictures.

Todd sent me one of his boot camp graduation pictures, and he looked great, so accomplished. I was proud for him, and for me, because I was only running a month behind him. Lenny's picture did raise questions from my nearby bunkmates, as everyone was curious as to why I had a picture of a blond-headed Marine and this other guy. I would simply say, "This is what you run to and this is what you run from." And then I would change the subject, because (1) it made me mad for anyone to comment on how nice looking Lenny was, and (2) we opened our mail in the open and I was afraid one of our sergeants might notice they had never seen me receive "that" picture in the mail, and then it would become contraband, like the hairbrush Miss Alabama had snuck in. I knew I wasn't giving up Lenny's picture. I had run away from him, but I wasn't free. He still mattered. I still prayed for him, and when I got still enough to think about it, I still longed for him. Lucky for me, "still" is not something you have much time allotted for in a Marine Corps Boot Camp.

I really hadn't considered how fully packed the days and nights would be. I hadn't gone into the recruiting offices or even asked Gunny how difficult boot camp might be. I had failed to ask things like, "How often will I get to make calls?" and "Will we get weekends off?" I now knew the answer would have been *none* to both of those particular questions. But even if he had told me—and looking back, he and some others may have tried—it wouldn't have changed my choice.

What I had endured, with my friends and family, in order to join *any* branch had been difficult, so why would I bother looking for an easy way to do it once I was in?

Besides, I liked a good challenge. I was born for it. Make it easy and I will sleep through it. Give me a time limit on a test, yes! Love it! It gives me a rush and I'll ace it! Tell me it is highly unlikely that anyone will make a C in Mr. Abney's class, oh yeah, I will end up with an A or B! And apparently, being told I COULDN'T or that I LACKED THE ABILITY to do something or to finish something, well, if I didn't get it done, expect to find me dead somewhere, because I was going to die trying! I don't have a quit button. Sometimes that's bad, but in boot camp, it worked to my favor.

So here I was, all in. I'd kind of figured out that the drill instructors were always going to be pushing you verbally and hollering. I just had to make sure I did what *had* to be done to the best of my ability. I still didn't like exercise, but I found I could make the three-mile in a little over twenty-two minutes by sprinting and walking. (The drill instructors didn't like that I just didn't run, but I got stitches in my side when I kept it all at a steady, heavy pace. If I sprinted half a lap and then power walked, I was good to go *and* not hurting during the rest of our PT time.) I could do twenty-five sit-ups, twenty-five push-ups, and fifteen chin-ups in the allotted time. I could tread in twelve-foot water while removing my boots and camouflaged jacket and turning the jacket into a life preserver and still keep kicking for thirty minutes.

I could break down an M-16 in the dark under time (that was fun!). I could step into the gas chamber and remove my mask and give an account of myself even as the gas was being released and in spite of the fact that we all knew Fulton was going to freeze up and we'd be stuck in there and smoked out.

I aced standard, prep, and classroom tests, even though I skipped study time on Sunday mornings to attend church. My bunk, my trunk, and my clothes were above reproach. My faith was full and holding. My pride in what I could do was skyrocketing!

I did catch slack after I asked my mom to send me pajamas, as I was freezing every night in my top bunk under the air conditioner vent, because she sent me the cutest white flannel pajamas with little red hearts on them—but I actually think the DIs were messing with me then. I think?

But when it came to my hair, that was another story. It was auburn. Yeah, you know that. It had some natural curl or frizz. I've told you that. It was long, long enough for me to pull up into a bun at the nape of my neck as I was supposed to; *however, no amount* of hairspray was going to keep *my* tresses from escaping! The DIs acted as if I was doing it on purpose to look cute for the male Marines who served us our meals, but we couldn't even make eye contact with them, so that seemed ludicrous to me. But one day, having just had another chewing out THIS RECRUIT asked for a pair of scissors and went to the back and cut my hair. That's what they kept telling me *they* were going to do, so I did it for them. Straight across at my jaw line! Regulation. And what happened next? They started fussing at me because I couldn't contain my short hair. (*Yeah*, you are kidding me! That's what I said, but I didn't say it out loud :o)

16

It was awesome to be part of a team that was being trained and given the privilege of serving our nation and preserving freedom. I loved the drills, especially the intricate ones where we all went different directions and crossed paths without ever interfering with each other's routes. I loved the pounding of our boots and the chants and songs we'd voice while marching. I loved how we had each other's back, and except for Fulton's insecurities popping up a couple of times, we didn't get into anything or leave anyone struggling alone. We either jumped in to do it together or we paid the price of not getting it done together. *Together.* It was the Corps. We were a team. And we became family. And I *loved* being a part of something so much bigger than myself.

As graduation loomed near, we went for final assessments and to find out what our jobs (aka MOSs) would be. I had been warned that because I wouldn't wait, I might be given something I would have never chosen, but I had accepted that and had been praying my way through it. Wherever I was needed and told to go THAT is where I would be.

But that's not exactly how it went down, as my testing scores, perfect pitch, and clean background opened up an intelligence area opportunity and they offered me a job. I was soooooo excited, but I simply responded, "Yes, I am interested."

Then they sent me in to another officer for further discussions about the job requirements. Then they lost me, and my mind was spinning—I might as well have signed up for submarine duty if I wasn't going to see the *real* sky. But I said nothing. He was locking eyes with me, and I was holding his gaze, not wanting to misunderstand anything. I knew by now that full attention was always part of the protocol. Then he asked me, "Feltrop, would you be willing to take on this assignment?"

I said, "Yes, sir," because I would have.

Then I surprised myself by speaking out of turn. "When you said I would be underground for a month, did that mean I would be in lockdown in a building or actually underground, sir?"

He looked at me and stated simply, "It would be the second."

To which I simply nodded and said, "Yes, sir."

I thought it was done, but then he asked me another question, "Private, is this something you would want to do?"

Still holding his gaze, I said, "It would not be my first choice, sir."

"But would the Marine do it?"

"Yes, sir."

Still having a starring match, he leaned in. "What is *it* the *prrrrivate* would like to do?"

I said without hesitation, "Anything outside, sir."

He studied me for a moment and I held his gaze. "You know,

of course that there are limited jobs outdoors for a female Marine and you could request something different but better than an outside job?"

"If possible, this Marine would just like to be outside, sir."

I was dismissed.

A couple of days later, I received a call to come into the drill instructor's office. Sergeant Pollet was on duty so I was flustered going in, because her saying my name never was a good thing. I actually thought I might be finding out where they had decided to place me, but that wasn't the case tonight.

It always seemed to start with questions "FELTROP. Did this recruit TELL her family she was NOT going home between graduation and her training assignment?"

"Yes, ma'am."

"And WHYYYYYY would the recruit not go home?" She sounded so bored, which meant she was fixing to explode, so I readied myself before I continued. Besides, I needed time to figure out the shortest way to explain this, as none of them were prone to liking lengthy answers.

"This recruit had to run away to enlist and was told *not* to come back home, ma'am."

"By whom were you told this, Private Feltrop?"

"By my father, ma'am."

Then she started but it was soft, not deafening. "Then can the RECRUIT ... tell ME ... why HER father spent a whole day consuming Marine Corps officials' time insistent upon talking to her? *Do* you know how much work that entails? How many people had to STOP what THEYYY were doing to handle your 'family matter'?"

"No, ma'am. The private didn't know they would—"

"STOP. THIS private will go home for a week after boot camp." Okay, here it came, her famous, overwhelming volume increase. "And THIS private ... IS going to get on THIS phone ... and simply state to whomever is on the other end ... 'I ... will ... be ... coming home.' And THEN dismiss herself *quickly* so I can get back to what I AM SUPPOSED to be doing."

I did it just like she said and scurried out of there.

Was everybody's life so messy? Shoot, even I knew *no one* could get hold of you during boot camp, so I was pretty sure my dad must have been causing a stink somewhere today, but I couldn't help them now.

Inside? Inside of me, I didn't know whether to be upset because Sergeant Pollet was angry with me again or cry because I could see my family or be scared at the thought of being face to face with my dad. So instead of thinking, I did what was now second nature to me: I busied myself writing a letter to Mom. I'm not sure why, but Todd and I had just kind of quit writing, and it didn't seem the other was overly concern. So with Mom's letter done, I read my Bible, and then I prayed, lying Lenny's picture under my palm. But it was different now. It was distant. I wasn't praying anymore for us. It didn't make sense to beat a dead horse, so to speak. I might be home for a week, but I would be gone three more years, so now I just prayed for him and I prayed for me, and I went to sleep.

ৎ৵

Two days went by. We had just returned from preparing for our graduation service when I got called back in to receive my MOS assignment. It was my misfortune that once again Sergeant Pollet was on duty. (*How* do I get so lucky?) So I readied myself as I walked halfway through the barracks to her office *again*.

And here we went. "Does the RECRUIT have her MOS assignment yet?"

Standing, as always when with an official, I responded *as always* loudly enough for ALL to hear. "NO MA'AM, this recruit does not have her MOS assignment yet." (She knew I didn't have it, because

THEY were the ones that were *supposed* to give it to me! But I didn't bat an eye OR say a word.)

"Well I AM SO SORRYYY (her sarcasm was soooo thick) didn't the Marine Corps offer you an MOS? WAITTT, I believe they did offer you an excellent opportunity. And what did the recruit say? Ohhh wait (boy, she was frustrated with me!!!) I have it here. The RECRUIT, Private Feltrop, deferred her request and is requesting ... an *outdoor* job." Then, sitting the paperwork aside, she continued, "Does THIS Marine understand that she is NOT in charge."

"Yes, Sergeant."

"Then why does MY recruit keep causing MY superiors such problems?"

Oh shoot! If she had got in trouble because of me, then I and the whole platoon would be in for some ditch digging in the sand in just a minute. I needed to back out and apologize for living and breathing and anything else I had done.

"This recruit did not intend to cause problems, Sergeant."

"Well then Missssss *Private Feltrop*, let me tell YOU what YOU did for yourself! You locked yourself into only two options: driving jarheads or MPing leathernecks. I don't believe you are equipped well for *either. However*, at my discretion, I have consulted with them and recommended that you *not* be given the MOS of MP (military police). *You are* tooooo soft Recruit to take on a drunken fight, and God forbid someone cuss at you and make ... you ... cry."

Yupppp she was trash-talking me, but everything she said was true.

She continued, "So, Marine, you have been assigned to Transportation."

She gave me details, but I heard nothing else except that I was dismissed. I felt immediately relieved but just a little flustered, because the more I had pondered it, the less I understood *why* I had felt so adamantly that I couldn't/shouldn't go underground. Dang, that was what I had signed up for, to be used to serve, and then when they told me how, I said *no*. No end to stupid. But it was done now, and so was boot camp—almost. A meeting to get my first check and next assignment and a short march would conclude this season of my life, and I was prouder of that than the twelve years of school, where I had invested so little. It didn't matter that I hadn't requested anyone to come to my graduation and there was no one in the crowd for me. I was under the sun and felt as noticed and loved, as I did on any day when I was walking on the hills with God.

ৡৢ

Even after paying for my uniforms and a ticket home, I still had more money in my hand than I had ever held before. But it couldn't compare to the pride I felt just in *doing* the thing everyone doubted I could. I had done all that was required to be called a Marine. So, as I loaded up, in my civilian clothes once again, and prepared for the long bus ride home, I was sitting quietly and content and only just a tad nervous. We had been warned right before leaving about practicing caution when traveling alone or at night, and it looked as if I was going to do both of the aforementioned. But then we got to Georgia, and in stepped a young man in uniform—a Marine. Okay now I felt safe, but I'd have felt safer if he was sitting by me, so I went back and introduced myself and asked him how far he was going. When he said Memphis, I asked him if he'd mind sitting by me, as I was traveling alone and headed into Little Rock.

He obliged, glad for the company, and we sat and visited. His name was Eric, a private first class just like myself, fresh out of boot camp. He was cute, sporting a dark brown military cut. My height. Sturdy built. It got late soon after he boarded, and people and towns came and went and we just kept talking. We talked about where we grew up, school, dating, boot camp, dreams, etc. By the time we hit Tennessee we were holding hands and exchanging numbers and addresses, and long before we got to Jackson we were making plans to meet in November and enjoy some kissing. In case you couldn't tell, I like kissing and being kissed. Eventually, I fell asleep with my head on his shoulder and he awoke me with a kiss as we were pulling into his stop. Grabbing his stuff, he said he'd call. And he did.

He even called that evening wanting to make sure everything had gone down all alright with my folks when they picked me up. The next night, I was going to be at my Aunt Mary's and Uncle Ken-ken's, so I gave him that number as well. Each time he called, I insisted we didn't need to talk long or he didn't have to call every night, as it was an expensive thing to do back in the day. (In the 1980s, long distance was *expensive!!*) But Eric insisted, and I enjoyed it. It made me eager to get back to the East Coast so I too could start my training and get on with my new life.

Everything had been good, not so smooth with my dad but good enough, and I only had a day left before I headed out. I had spent the night with Gunny and Mrs. Becky the night before. I was taking a long cut home by Dandy Don's to get a Coke when I pulled over to talk with Ricky near the corner of Main and Race. That's when Lenny showed up. All of the sudden, Ricky was leaving and I was left with him. Honestly, a part of me wanted to take off but I wasn't going to run like I was scared. Yet there he sat in his Camaro, looking the same and smelling the same—good. (You know, you really shouldn't be able to smell someone's cologne when they are sitting in another vehicle, but you always could Lenny's.)

I thought I felt confident enough to handle whatever he said this time. Besides, I had Eric so how much could this hurt. My world didn't revolve around him; it had expanded greatly since July. But he checked me pretty quick. He didn't say, "Congrats on finishing" or anything positive, just a bunch of questions and one statement.

First: "How long are you in town?" While it wasn't how I expected him to start our conversation, it wasn't as bad as how our last one had ended. In fact, he sounded like the guy I'd dated. Hmmm.

"I leave tomorrow.'"

"Where are you headed? Maybe I'll come see you." Well I had
not anticipated this, but I probably should have.

"It'd be a long drive, because I am headed to North Carolina
for more training."

"When will you be back?" Here we go. This sounded more like
the guy I had spoken to before I left, not near so as friendly.

"I won't know until I get there."

Yuppp and that was it for Mr. Nice Guy, as his next question
came in hot. "Where's my jersey?"

This time I had it in my trunk, and I couldn't think of one
reason to hang onto it. Sooooo, I got out and tossed it to him. I
didn't throw it. (See how much self-control I had gained?☺

Then, realizing he was playing *my* Michael Jackson cassette, I
asked for *it* back. He popped it out and tossed it back to me.

Here it came again, another Cold War, which neither of us
intended to lose, but as he started his car to pull out, he won the
battle with a final sentence. "I hate your haircut." Then he was gone,
tearing off down the street.

I fumed all the way home but talked to Eric about it when he
called and felt better. It wasn't until after that that my brother told
me he'd seen Lenny a couple of times while I was gone and that
he'd been asking about me. Well, that sounded different than the
impression he always gave me, and I did spend some time thinking
about it as I repacked to head out, especially when I grabbed my
Bible. For a moment I thought about taking his picture out of my
Bible; after all, I wasn't praying for us every day anymore. We weren't
in love. We didn't have a future. But I didn't. I left it in my Bible.
Closed it up tightly so it couldn't fall out and loaded it back into
my luggage.

And I went to bed ... but not to sleep.

୨୦ ୧୬

I was soooo mad at him. I didn't have a right to be. This was soooo
stupid! A grown woman not able to keep her feelings in check! Not
able to define why she was even in such a rage! And I was extremely,
EXTREMELY angry! Helplessly I kept trying to get my mind to shift
direction onto anything else, but it just kept coming back to the same
thing. Lenny. So I turned on and up the music hoping to drown it all off
with some Journey, but the stupid machine kept kicking off or turning
it down! I got up a third time to fix it. I had to be dreaming. This had
to be a nightmare, because nothing made sense. I slammed the door, but
what I wanted to do was hit something! What in the world was going
on? This wasn't me. I didn't hit stuff when I was upset. But I not only
wanted to hit something; I was using a ton of profanity in my mind,
and I didn't do that either! I sounded like a two-day-in drunk Marine!

It was getting darker by the minute. Lenny was out enjoying
himself and I was trapped. He was out where I would expect
him to be, but I seemed to be expecting something different …
something different! There was absolutely NO reason for me to
be feeling like this, but it had been creeping in all day. My chest
hurt! My whole body was knotted up. My teeth set and clenched.

I couldn't sit anymore. None of these feelings made sense. The
next thing I knew, I was in the truck, and then as soon as I got
passed people, I cranked the music, burnt rubber, just letting it fly
and trying to lose whatever was holding me! My mind, my heart,
my head, my body was sooooooo tense, racked with crazed chaos.
How long could a person scream without making a sound!

I was losing my mind … surely, I could wake up.

Just calm down. Exhale. Maybe it would all go away. Just breathe …

Breathe …

17

I appreciated the fact that my new career left me exhausted by 9:30 and ready to crash not long after, because if I was physically exhausted I was also probably dreamless, and that was a good thing these days.

Having landed at Camp Geiger, it didn't take long for things to kind of fall into a routine, with one obvious difference. There were less than two dozen girls in our dorm sharing the same amount of space the five dozen of us had squeezed into at boot camp. Sweet!

In the morning we'd walk across to school for training. Have classes and drive five to eight hours and work on learning preventive maintenance stuff. Then I'd split off to grab a bite at the canteen for supper as I still disliked lunch rooms, a.k.a., chow halls. To conclude

my day, I'd go to *my* pay phone booth (mine simply because that
was the only one I had given Eric the number to), and we'd talk an
hour or so each night. Then bed. Then it would all start again the
next morning. It wasn't bad; in fact, I actually ended up with three
girls with me from boot camp, so I knew faces.

Our job would be transportation, which meant we would be
trained to drive and do routine maintenance on everything up to a
5-ton. Our class was filled with people right out of boot camp, about
four to five dozen of us, primarily males. It didn't take me long to
be grateful my dad had made me learn to drive the hard way—in
a standard rather than an automatic, parked halfway up a steep
country road instead of on a cul de sac. That was working to my
benefit now, because I was ace-ing the driving! However, there were
about a half-dozen in our class that had never driven at all and over
a dozen who had never worked a clutch. They were having a totally
different experience those first few weeks.

We all got to know each other pretty quick, but gone was the
kumbaya spirit of boot camp. The girls were back to acting like
high schoolers. Drinking, doing drama, and even dipping chew!
Disgusting! In fact, the two prettiest girls were the worst. I don't
think it helped anything that our home base ratio was like one girl
for every forty to fifty guys! But they often acted like desperate
females, and I just couldn't get it and totally disliked the strain and
cliqueness that could often be felt in the barracks. I just wanted to
stay out of the middle of their stuff.

There was, however, one girl there whom I actually didn't see
until I had been there for days. Her bunk was in the back corner, so
you couldn't see it as you walked in because it was usually dark on
that end as we all slept on the other end by the TV and bathrooms.
The first time I saw her, after I jumped back scared because I thought
I was alone (yikes!), she was perched on the top bunk. She was a
young, slender black girl with thick glasses surrounded by a dozen
or more books, reading. I smiled and introduced myself and she

quietly, *very* quietly told me her name. She was in the unit ahead of us and had actually been here for weeks. I apologized for not seeing her and then made a joke about her maybe having the best location, as she wasn't close enough to hear or feel the drama. She just nodded without saying anything. Yeah! I am assuming she liked it less than me, because she *never ever* came around any of us or spoke to us. She was probably pretty nice, but by never speaking or smiling, she came off kinda spooky.

Anywayyyys I remained friendly with as many as I could, even the guys. I always found it interesting to hear someone else's story and life and there were plenty around to hear. But people, you know we always tell people what we'd *like* them to know. It's when we'd be hanging out at the canteen after hours that you learned the rest by watching what "wasn't" said or shared. You learned who had the foul mouths. Who was a "lady's man." The jokester, who liked to drink but who shouldn't drink at all because they could not hold their liquor.

I also learned that while they had Sunday services on base, only two guys and no girls seemed interested in going. Several things made the situation difficult: the guys were not on my end of the base; nor were the churches. What to do? In boot camp, I had gone to the Protestant service that encompassed all "Christian" churches: Baptist, Church of Christ, Assembly, Methodist, etc. Another thing that made this hard was that these two great guys were both of different faiths than I was. Super nice! But one was Jewish and one was Catholic, and I was not comfortable rotating services and too broke for a taxi, so I never started church. (My first and probably biggest mistake as there is accountability in a church family, not so much in our Marine Corps family... Just saying.)

In two weeks we got our first full paycheck (without transportation expenses), and then I learned the most troubling thing of all. I knew a lot of the girls had dates and were going to be gone all weekend. But I didn't know until I went in late Friday night after talking with Eric that *all* of them were going to be gone! So I spent Saturday hanging around the canteen with the wise ones, broke ones (from repaying all the money they had borrowed since they arrived), and married ones, who had the majority of their monies sent home to their families. Saturday night, Eric and I visited for hours since no one was around to need the phones, and that night it was just me again. Well, there was also the girl in the corner, but that didn't make me feel more comfortable.

It wasn't until everybody started showing back up that I realized we had another difference. Curiosity compelled me to ask, "Where did ya'll all go?" Awwww yuppp I still remember the knowing glances.

Ferg, my bunkmate in boot camp, was the one who answered. "The guys got paid and were willing to pay for the weekend so I took off."

In my naivety, I just kept asking questions but this time more quietly. "But where do you stay when ya'll go off?"

She smiled and arched her eyebrows at me, I believe she was enjoying watching my shock "WE stay ALONE with our dates in nice hotel rooms with pools and bathtubs." My mind raced ahead, and then it hit me—the guys paid the bill and the girls paid their end with services rendered. I *know* she saw it in my eyes as it clicked in, because she just kinda laughed. I was trying to make it better by establishing some kind of relationship between her and her soldier, but NOPE there hadn't been and wouldn't be, as she had met someone else while they were out.

Ohhhh great! Yuppppp I just got a little sick to my stomach and felt a little nasty, but I said nothing. I just walked back toward my bunk area to my locker, pretending I was looking for something, but all I was actually doing was trying to find something redeemable in their situation. But Ferg would have none of it and followed me back around the lockers, still talking. She actually invited me to join her next weekend, because the other guy she'd met was actually a lieutenant and had a friend.

I was thinking a lot of things, but all I said was "You are going to get busted for being with an officer."

I turned away then swinging open my locker door, gathering my laundry and hoping my fast friend would head back around to where she had been before. But she just laughed a little and said, "I'll only get in trouble *if* I get caught, and I *don't* get caught."

I tried not to let her see my disgust. She was using them for their money. They were using her for sex! She had no morals. She had no fidelity or bent toward faithfulness, recruiting a new date while she out with the other one! She had no respect for authority. Lowly enlisted people *could not even* date officers *or* upper enlisted personnel. I just *didn't* get it. And suddenly I just wanted back the space I had had Saturday night.

But that didn't happen; in fact, she stepped forward to examine the picture taped to my locker door.

Her next words caught me off guard. "Is that Eric?"

As my mind was still racing, I glanced over at the only picture in my locker and caught her examining him. I didn't like her look AT ALL! and fought the urge to close the door with her face still in it (yeah, see what a week of not getting my spiritual tank filled does to me?), but I didn't, not even when she started in on him being so cute and how she wanted to meet him when he came in next month. Yeah – NO! That was not going to happen.

I had had a cousin that looked and lived liked Ferg (tall, energizing, not pretty but strikingly beautiful). I hadn't been actually able to tell her who I really liked for the past two years, because that just always turned out to be the one I found her flirting with when I went back into work. So, no! I knew I wouldn't be introducing Ferg to anybody! But I didn't have to worry about her meeting this fellow. Almost angry due to her attention to him, I let her know ASAP that this guy was NOWHERE around where we were and she wouldn't be meeting him because that was a guy from back home! Definitely not a Marine!

I don't know why I thought that would end it, but I closed the door to find her staring at me.

Cocking her head, she smiled slyly. "So when Eric shows up in November, should I tell him you have some other guy's picture in your locker?" *Oooooooo*, that sounded almost like a threat. But I wasn't too worried and simply responded flatly, unwilling to let her make me angry or lose my temper, "You could, but I'd rather you not. You are already hanging out with more men than you can handle. Why don't you focus on that?"

I'm not sure I had ever been that worked up. I could have gotten into a cat fight. What had happened to the Jesus in me? I know what happened. Just like in any relationship, when you quit showing up for dates, you find yourself alone. I had quit showing up. I was AWOL—Absent With Out Leave! And I was acting like it! Now I wasn't just disappointed in her. *Now* I was mad at *me*!

And she walked away laughing.

I knew I should probably go ahead and tell Eric because Ferg— even though she and I were friends— and I we were so different that she might just tell him. I tossed it over and back a hundred ways while I sat outside enjoying the sunset and the coolness that had swung in over the weekend. Looking at my watch, I saw I still had thirty minutes before Eric's eight o'clock call, and I decided I would tell him about Ferg but not about the exchange that occurred over the photo. When I got home, I'd just take it down. Odds were she and Eric wouldn't meet when he came in anyway.

But I hadn't finished concreting my plans when another problem showed up, named RJ. Well, I wouldn't actually call him a problem. In fact, I had been grateful he had been around the past few days to hang out with and visit with while all my roommates were gone.

He had a friendly disposition and was fun and funny. His hair was, of course, in a GI cut but was a light to medium brown. We were all in shape, but he was leaner, not stocky built. This past week, we female Marines had been instructed not to walk alone after dark, so this weekend, RJ had volunteered to walk me back to the barracks from the canteen, and when he realized I was not going in but sitting outside at the phone booths for a call from my boyfriend, RJ had waited with me, even hanging around until I was done and then escorting me to the base of my barracks. I had told him it wasn't necessary, but he had said he had nothing else to do so he just hung back for an hour or so smoking and waiting and occasionally cutting up.

However, with everyone back on base and me not coming from the canteen (because my conversation with Ferg had left me to nauseated to eat), I was shocked to see him there. I did, however, appreciate that he was watching my back and jokingly told him he was released from his duties as my night guard. Thanking him, I told him that my side of the campus was repopulated, as most of the girls were already back from their rendezvous so he could go back to hanging with his buddies, but he just smiled and sat down next to me. I didn't mind too much, as his lightheartedness was a blessed distraction from the previous hours' junk. But then it started feeling as if he were half-flirting. I thought he was either joking because he sensed my stress or had been drinking. And I probably should have insisted but didn't attempt to send him on his way again. What did it matter? Hadn't he sat there and listened to my half of our private conversation two nights already, *so* he knew who Eric was, where Eric was, and that he was territorial and that he was coming in November to see me and bring me an engagement ring. (Yeah, we were moving pretty fast for kids who'd only sat together for a ten-hour bus trip. Look at me! Did you really think I was going to start making sense now? Sorry, it takes a looooong time to work through some kinds of stupid.) But I did think I might want to remind RJ, in case he had been drinking, that he had to be quiet. I didn't need him getting Eric worked up, as he was so certain some Marine was going to steal me away.

RJ just sat and smiled when I called him on his sassy attitude and he told me not to worry, as he was just messing with me. Then we visited like normal, until Eric called. When the phone rang, he jumped up and helped me to my feet, and I waved him goodbye and turned into the booth. Eric was still talking when I shifted around ten to fifteen minutes later to find RJ still around. He was standing in his normal place, about ten feet over, smoking at the edge of the grass until he saw me looking at him then he stepped on his cigarette. I still didn't like smoking or drinking around me, so I appreciated his consideration for me. But now he was done and headed over my way. Then he started being completely stupid and trying to tickle me, and I couldn't get him to go away and I was struggling not to laugh. But it tickled and he was stupidly endearing.

Realizing RJ was being successful at distracting me, I turned back around and stepped as far into the phone booth as I could in order to clear my mind and to focus on mine and Eric's conversation. I needed to share that "stuff" that had gone down earlier with Ferg, but I was struggling with the picture thing still—feeling as if I should tell him and yet feeling as if he wouldn't find out anyway. Actually, mentioning Lenny would just get him worked up when there wasn't even anything there to worry about.

I was still chasing that rabbit in my head when RJ stepped into the phone booth with me and closed the door. Those things were not made to be comfortable for two adults who didn't want to be cozy. RJ didn't seem to mind, but I *did*. *That was it* for me today. I couldn't handle one … more … thing! And the glance I gave him should have melted him, but he didn't leave. Just smiled and leaned against the glass.

So now I wasn't talking at all just encouraging Eric to talk while I shifted gears from Ferguson and Lenny to my more immediate issue. In case you are young and didn't know, you can't open a phone booth door when someone is leaning on it from the inside! And to make matters worse, he kept whispering stupid stuff to me. If Eric had been the one I was hearing say it, I would have called it sweet, but Eric and I were dating and RJ and I were *not*! Not cool at all, and it wasn't long before Eric heard a man's voice and then I just flat-out told him a lie. "The phones are swamped tonight and it is just the folks in line waiting." I slid off as quickly as possible, because I didn't want to know if he was buying it or not (remember, I am a poor liar). I could tell from his voice he was getting riled, so that was my safest option anyway.

With that done, I turned to RJ, not smiling at all, and told him to open the door, which he did with much gallantry, and I rudely brushed past him straight up and into the barracks. Opening the locker to make sure I was ready for Monday morning, I saw Lenny looking back at me, but I didn't take the picture down I was mentally done sparring with people for the night, even if one of those people happened to be me.

18

I didn't think any phone conversation could go worse, but the next night did. As RJ was in my phone booth BEFORE I got back from having supper. He also refused to leave, but with much ado he offered to let *me* join *him* in order to take Eric's call. Yuppp and now Eric wasn't buying it that it was all people *outside* the booth. Soooo … I told him. He got angry and asked to speak to RJ and I let him. Eric threatened and RJ smiled. And when Eric asked if he had left, RJ opened the door but remained. And I lied again and then tried to carry on, as if I was alone. Not my best moment; I was on some kind of roll!

Yeah that was how the week ran, all week! No matter what time I went to the phone booth, RJ was always there. He was as exasperating as Lenny had been- in that EVERY time I tried to stepped forward, there he was. The folks in our training group thought it was funny, and when I told them that when Eric showed up to get me he was going after RJ first. I thought they'd reason with him, but instead they said if *anyone* went after RJ, he'd have a dozen Camp Geiger Marines on his back.

I just didn't see how I was going to win even when Eric upped the stakes by proposing we get married Veteran's Day. RJ heard it and shot me back a questioning glance. When I told Eric yes, RJ left on his own accord. Then Eric and I discussed what it might look like afterwards while we waited on our orders to merge and how long we would wait before having a family and even life after our enlistments. He'd bring the rings with him. He loved me, he said, and his last words that night were "Hold on."

The next night, however, we were back to our new norm, as RJ beat me to the phone booth again.

The problem was I didn't eat breakfast. I ate a lil' bag of chips and a soda most days for lunch, and so *of course* I was at the canteen ready for my chicken steak sandwich or popcorn shrimp basket as soon as they opened. I had to eat! This six-foot chick had a hard time keeping her weight up to 140. I may have had a few curves, but I was too darn skinny, and supper was my only real meal, so NO … I wasn't going to race him to the booth at six for a call that wouldn't come until eight. And after a couple of days, I even quit hurrying, showing up early as I knew RJ would be there holding my spot. At least he had quit trying to talk while Eric was on the line. He talked before and he tried to talk after but he was quiet while we talked. A few days later, a gift came for me from Tennessee. Eric had had a shirt made for me that said 'ERIC'S' on the back and that sported an armed Marine Corp bulldog on the front that said HANDS OFF. I thought it was sweet. RJ thought it was funny. I warned him that Eric was larger framed and that I thought his best bet was to leave me alone before Eric showed up and cleaned his plow!

That night, as RJ laughed, all I could see was Eric beating the mess out of him *or* a bunch of our friends rallying behind RJ and tearing into Eric. I didn't like any of it, because I *don't* like drama—girl drama or boy drama—and fighting was just boy drama.

So I just asked him, "RJ, what's it going to take to get you out of here? Out of this booth tonight. Tomorrow night. Next week."

He looked up at me with no laughter in his eyes, just intent, and then actually stepped out of the booth. For a minute, he simply stared toward the canteen, and then he looked back at me where I was leaning against the phone booth door, arms crossed and waiting.

Then he said, "Go out with me. If you don't like me more than him after our date, then I'll leave you two alone."

Sounded doable. So I agreed that IF he left *immediately*, I'd go out with him Sunday to the movie on base.

He left.

I was going to tell Eric all the details, but he was in a temper when he called, not trusting that RJ wasn't hanging around. I just told him I had handled it and changed the subject to his arrangements for joining me in a few weeks. Once things chilled out and since we were actually alone we could enjoy a more relaxed and intimate conversation. In two weeks, we'd be together and married. But even as we talked, my mind kept trying to interrupt and lay guilt on me about the RJ thing. I seemed to be collecting secrets from Eric and that didn't feel right morally—at all.

Then I caught a flashback in my mind of Ferg at my locker when we had had the exchange about her flipping fellas and how disgusted I had been. It was followed by a picture of me and RJ in the phone booth while I was talking to Eric. That was quickly followed by my daily thoughts about the man in the photo that *still* hung in my locker. How different was I than Ferg? The problem was that my heart kept convincing me that the only difference was that I was a virgin. *Ouch.*

I finished the call, emotionally exhausted from trying to corral my thoughts so I could visit with Eric and dream out loud. I wanted to love someone. I wanted to be loved. I wasn't looking for one-night stands. I wanted a lifetime together being adored by *one* man. And no, I didn't tell Eric about my arrangement with RJ. I'd handle RJ on my own, and if he pulled any stunts, I would be sure to have money for a taxi home.

Done for the day, I made my way slowly upstairs, exhausted not physically but in every other way you could be. Opening my locker door, I looked right into Lenny's face and then slammed it shut, giving up on doing one more thing and opting to sleep in my T-shirt. I dropped the boots and camis and flung back the covers. I was mad. Once again I was tired and flustered!

I whispered into the dark, "Maybe all men are vain, selfish jerks!"

But as I climbed into bed to lay down and try to pray, I was interrupted by an all too familiar Voice, which said, "Maybe you are the 'jerk.' You are thinking you'll marry one, going on a date with another, *and* yet your heart is still hanging in your locker."

Ouch! That shut me up. I didn't say anything else, including my prayers, because I knew I was getting it all messed up, and what do you say? What excuse do you present to the God who knows the hidden things of your heart?

Friday was payday and a couple of us girls pooled our money after class for a ride to the PEMEX. I, with much embarrassment, bought a negligee for my wedding night. I was a bit scared and nervous, because I knew little about those things (i.e., sex). Okay, I knew almost nothing except it would hurt pretty bad and you would bleed the first time. So now sex was weighing on my mind and had been all afternoon since I had made a doctor's appointment for Monday so I could get on birth control. Nothing the receptionist said I would need to do at the doctor's office sounded enjoyable *at all*, but as our plan was not to have kids until we were able to be stationed together, it was necessary. I had hoped the purchase of the negligee would help me regain the romantic hue to the upcoming events. It didn't, but talking with Eric later that night and the next did.

Saturday night, I told Eric to call me early Sunday afternoon, as I was going out with Tina and some friends but in reality that was ANOTHER lie. I just needed him not to call so I could get this thing with RJ wrapped up. Hearing I had gotten the other things done, he didn't seemed concerned at all, and for the first time in almost two weeks he didn't ask where RJ was. Our wedding date was ten days out. I just needed to get this date done.

Sunday evening, I was ready at six and we met at the canteen. RJ was already there in his civilian wear. Most days we just stayed in our camis as often as not, but *not* tonight, and that altered my ability to see it as a job rather than a date, which is what it had been in my mind all week. We sat, ate, and visited as two civilians would. I was once again appreciative that he was still being considerate of my feelings about alcohol and smoking and didn't partake in either.

As we headed out he opened the door and we walked into the darkness, the conversation was just ... wonderful! Not at all like the heavy ones Eric and I had been having lately. I found this quite refreshing, and as much as I hated to admit it, I was really enjoying the walk. That camaraderie was what had made RJ and I good enough friends for me to have even asked for his help a couple of weeks prior. I missed that. Fun. Friendly engagement. Maybe it wasn't even Eric's fault I wasn't enjoying our visits lately; maybe it was me still wrestling with my conscious ... okayyyyyy I wasn't thinking about that now. I just wanted to focus on one thing at a time, and right now that was RJ and the task at hand. And gosh, he was being so polite! He wasn't even flirting. This wasn't bad at all. He was just fun and relaxing to be around.

I had my first blah moment when we finally arrived at the movie and, ugh, it's James Bond. You know it's frustrating constantly being taken to a movie that *only* the guy is gonna like, but here I was again. Oh well, it makes sense that a base filled with guys would show a guy movie, so I could get over it. RJ paid to get us in and for the popcorn! Love it! I was grateful for my popcorn once the movie started, because I used it to keep RJ from holding my hand. However, I didn't fudge on his putting his arm around me unless it came over my shoulder. (You don't embarrass a guy too bad in front of his peers. At least this Marine wasn't going to do it to a fellow Marine.)

Afterwards I didn't call a taxi. He had not been pushy, so when he volunteered to walk me home, I said yes. It was a mile or so back to my end of the base, but he didn't push the touching whatsoever as we headed out. As we walked, we did have some pretty serious talk about life and a possible war as the Marine base in Beirut had been bombed recently. Then, stopping to let a car pass, he just leaned down and kissed me, and I let him. A kiss was always kind of my indicator because if it didn't feel right, it was soooo easy to say No. But as soon as he kissed me, he took off with my hand in his walking again. Talking. Laughing.

There weren't any other incidents as we walked on past the canteen, but when we got to the lawn by the barracks, he rolled the hand that held mine behind me and wrapped his other arm over my shoulder and really kissed me. It probably wasn't the right thing to do, but I tried to feel something. RJ was way easier to talk too than Eric. Much more comforting. Funny. Not so intense all the time. But as hard as I tried, I just couldn't. Well, he did make it way easier by interrupting and ending what could have been a very romantic kiss with more talking. He went back to conversing as if nothing had happened as we finished the walk to the barracks, standing around for another fifteen to twenty minutes, visiting. He didn't try to kiss me again, and so I assumed he must have gotten a "no" as well. I thanked him as I headed upstairs.

Pausing at the landing, I jokingly reminded him that he had

given his word not to show back up at my phone booth. Even in the dark, he looked a little funny, but I saw him nod—I think.

I thought it was all good and was congratulating myself, but I was wrong.

It was all fixing to blow up on me.

Everything!

19

Monday morning, I went to work and then after lunch took off to the doctor glad I had an appointment as I wasn't feeling well anyway. I told him I was tired and running a fever and couldn't shake a cough that had been worsening since hanging out with RJ in the damp air the night before. He said I had strep throat and a touch of bronchitis, then wrote me a script and a slip to miss work for the rest of the week and started to send me on my way until I reminded him that the actual reason I had requested an appointment was, because I needed to be put on birth control.

Since he didn't have any paperwork showing I'd had a "real" female checkup, he insisted on doing another so his records would be complete. He was flustered because he thought he was done already and then didn't have *any* of the paperwork. I was uncomfortable, as this was the first time I'd had a male doctor. I just was trying to focus on the picture above my head and breathe in and out and get it done when I felt an incredibly sharp, intense pain. Then he asked me, "Do you bleed like this every time you have sex?"

I responded, "I haven't ever had sex. I was getting on the pill because I am getting married in a week." Then we both got quiet.

I didn't even realize until I picked my medicine up that he had not given me a script for birth control. I was ashamed, as if I had done something. I was weak from my fever running over a hundred all day, and I was tired and broken. I wept all the way back to the bunkhouse. The one thing I had held onto and protected, even from someone I truly was ready to share myself with, was lost during a medical exam. Lost ...

When I got to my bunk I put on my flannel pajamas and set my alarm for 7:50 p.m. Everybody who used the phone booths knew I got a call at eight and was gracious enough to use one of the others or wait, so there was no need to go down too early. I just wanted to talk to Eric, tell him I was sick and go back to bed.

When the alarm went off, I didn't even bother dressing but wrapped a military wool blanket around my pajamas, trying not to wake up enough to start thinking and headed down to the phone booth. I wasn't even conscious of making the flights of stairs or crossing the lot. I wasn't conscious of anything until I gazed up to find someone in my booth: RJ.

"Are you okay? They said you were sick and might have to go stay at the infirmary." He was sincere, worried, gentle, and considerate. I was NOT.

"RJ, pleeeeease go away. I went on a date with you. You said you'd stop this. So stop." My voice was barely more than a whisper. I was hurting so bad. I should have stayed in bed. I just wasn't up for this.

But he continued anyway, "Yeah, but you kissed me."

"Yes, RJ, but I didn't feel anything when I kissed you. I tried. I'm sorry."

"But, Sherry, we—"

"But *we* nothing, RJ. I am getting married in nine days, and you need to go. I'm sick, and I'm not playing or trying to be friends tonight." Then we had a stare-down under the parking lot light fixtures, in *my* booth. He was looking at me with questions.

Me? My eyes were feverish, tear-stained, and lifeless. That had been my day. When the phone rang, I didn't reach around him or break his gaze. I just stood there looking at him like he was in the way - because he was. And I wasn't playing anymore. PERIOD. The phone quit ringing, and I was too tired to care. When it started again, he grabbed it up and turn his back to me. I assumed he was trying to play cat and mouse with me like he had done in the past. I just stood there and did nothing, waiting.

Then to my horror he started talking. "Eric, you need to know Sherry and I went out last night. She won't be marrying you. She is marrying me."

I couldn't believe my ears. I could feel myself falling. A Marine who visited with someone at another booth nightly stepped in and forced RJ to give me the phone. By then, Eric was hollering at me, and I was leaning against the cool glass of the booth while my new friend held RJ at arm's length so I could try to fix it. But I couldn't.

It didn't matter what we had planned or if RJ was lying about me marrying him.

The date wasn't a lie and I didn't deny it.

And when Eric asked if I had let RJ kiss me, I didn't lie about that either.

Then he hung up.

I waited hoping he'd call back.

So did RJ, but my unknown Marine friend did not.

But Eric didn't call back.

No words were spoken between RJ and me; nor did either of us move as the next ten minutes crept by. I was so weak. So sick. In my head. My heart. I'd had a horrific day planning for an event that wasn't even going to happen. I had lost the gift I had wanted to give the man who would love me forever. I was numb. And with no tears or emotion, all I could say as I pushed up and past him toward the barracks was, "RJ, thanks."

I have no idea what he was thinking, but he followed me, breaking the silence. "You didn't need to marry him. I went and bought a ring Saturday. Marry me."

I paused on the stairs for only a moment. "RJ, if you have a ring, you need to take it back and get a refund. Goodnight." And I went to bed and slept for three days straight, running a high fever and praying the meds they gave me would jump in and get me back on my feet.

I wouldn't be back in class at all that week. When I'd wake up I'd find my mind locked in the chaos of my life, tired of fighting my darkness I'd welcome sleep and the nightmares that had returned. Alone. In danger. Without a voice. Once again I was surrounded.

They haunted me all week and all weekend as I slept and sat in the stillness of the almost empty dorm. I was angry. And I was mad, and every time I thought about the last week's events – NO, the last year's junk—every time I looked at Lenny's picture, the silent tears would start anew. By Saturday night I was up and around, and I took Lenny's picture off my locker. I guess I should have tossed it but instead I put it back in the Bible that I had not opened in weeks.

That day I worked myself into a rage. I was NOT going to spend my life like I was helpless being picked up or led away by selfish men. (1) This would be my last weekend sitting here alone. (2) I had nothing to lose anymore. From now on I would be the one doing the choosing and the walking, without getting my heart entangled.

And this is what happens when a believer steps out of church and away from God. And this is what happens when a woman thinks that her purity is defined by her virginity rather than her desire for innocence.

 formula

Monday, I kept walking right past RJ and my friends on the field, at work and again in the canteen. I did look around and walk straight to up to the guy from another unit who seemed to think he was above all that and visited with him during our break.

My guy friends warned me he wasn't my type, but I didn't even know what that meant anymore. I thought Eric was. I thought RJ couldn't be. I had thought *actually* that the guy that been hanging in my locker was not my type, and he was the one I couldn't shake. That night, I sought the Marine Corp player out at the canteen. The next night, I dressed up in the brown suede skirt that favored me, with heels and a snug sweater. That night he asked me to join him Thursday night, and I said yes.

Everybody was shocked. Even Ferguson tried to stop me. Everyone wanted to know what happened with Eric. Everybody told me to wait.

"It's all the meds they had you on, Sherry. You aren't thinking clearly."

"What about RJ? If you are going out with somebody, go with someone who cares for you."

The problem was I didn't care anymore. About me. About RJ or Eric. Somehow *everybody* seemed to "know" I had been a virgin, and I think they thought they were protecting me, and I *wasn't* going to share about what had happened at the doctor's office. I wasn't going to tell them anything different.

Ferguson was having a fit, because I wouldn't change my mind. Begging. Reasoning with me. But I felt nothing and finally looked her in the eyes and said softly and cynically, "Maybe we are *not* so different. By the way, the guy's name that was on the picture in my locker is Lenny. The picture is stuffed in my Bible. Feel free to take it."

The next two weeks were a drunken blur, but I never took a sip of anything. My meds were finally done. I wasn't sick, but I wasn't whole. I slept with three men on three weekends, none of whom I cared for or who cared for me. I had no shame. I felt nothing. If sex was supposed to be so incredible, I was missing it. Shallow and hollow, that's how it left me. It did not feel empowering; it just felt pointless. I lost the respect of my peers, but I'd already lost respect for myself. Eventually even RJ left me alone. When my cycle started, I found myself faced with the silence of a quiet weekend again.

I fought a conscience that nagged and weighed on me until eventually I struck out for the canteen long after dark. It was actually against regulation for a female to be out alone after dark because of issues revolving around the squadrons of men housed on our base just in from the Beirut bombing. But I was still trying to run my own show and did it anyway.

It was way more crowded than usual, especially outside, but I got in all right only to find none of my old friends were there. If I had been thinking I would have called an MP to pick me up, but I hadn't thought much at all lately, and sadly that didn't change as I headed out the side door closest to my barracks where two to three dozen Marines were spread out drinking and very, very drunk.

I tried to show no fear, and I was a six-foot-tall chick, so I just stood up straighter and pressed through the dark, hoping that the shadows would camouflage me. I had almost made it to the road when I was caught from behind and slung to the ground. The next few moments were horrific. I thought I was screaming, but I couldn't hear a sound except their comments about what they were going to do. Kicking and trying to break free, I found one man holding my hands captive above my head while another straddled me, trying to unleash my belt, and another held my legs. I looked to the sides for help and saw two men watching, but neither moved to help. They were just watching. Bizarre zombies. Standing lifeless with filth flashing across their blinded eyes. Suddenly the hands got tired of their attempts to release my belt and reached up, grabbing and ripping my shirt.

Then came my silent cry, just like in my nightmares.

I was trapped.

It was hopeless.

I was alone.

And I had no voice as I faced my enemy and the minutes slipped by.

Danger had descended everywhere, but this wasn't a dream; it was a living nightmare.

God, help me! I screamed it in my heart even as I tried to grab air.

Then I heard a familiar voice demand, "Get off of her."

Looking back at him, they hurried to obey. They backed up from me. I balled up immediately trying to cover my breast. Afraid, so very afraid. Then he said with authority, "Give me your hand. I'm taking you home."

I looked back toward them when I realized he was alone, but the offenders simply stood in the shadows, still at attention. Then I looked at him, but it was not a face I knew. I didn't see rank or metal or even an MP wrap revealing what gave him power. But when he started walking toward my barracks, I walked at his side.

I raced to keep up to his long strides. Upon arriving at the base of the stair, he told me with the same authority, "Go upstairs and stay." And I took off, still shaking inside and out. It wasn't until I reached the door that I realized I hadn't said thank you. Turning around, I looked over the edge. But no one was there. The parking lot. The phone booths. The field we had just crossed—all were empty.

Quickly I went inside and locked the door as racking spasms of fear raced through my body. I went and showered, throwing the torn shirt and bra into the trash. Scrubbing anyplace where faces and hands had held, touched, and groped me.

Passing a mirror on my way to my bed, I jumped, startled. It took me several seconds to realize it was me—it didn't even look like me. Stepping closer, I looked at my face and closer into my eyes. There was nothing I recognized from the girl who had come on base just eight weeks earlier. What had I done?

What had I done?

With tears welling up again, I raced to my area, digging through my mess of a locker until I found my Bible. Then I turned to the verse I had memorized as a youth. Psalm 121:1-2, "I will lift up my eyes until the hills—from whence cometh my help? My help comes from the *Lord* ..." Lying in the floor, I wept in repentance and surrender until I could cry no more.

I was thankful it was time to leave this place. But even more than that, I was grateful. Grateful for a God who guarded me in my willfulness, offering once again forgiveness and second chances.

He spoke into the silence words of comfort and confirmation. "I love you. Your past is gone. Let it go. It doesn't matter, Sherry. It just doesn't matter."

And peace swept in with His Presence, wrapping me in arms of love and mercy.

I was here, but I was home.

20

With fresh orders in my hands I loaded the bus again, but this time I was unafraid. I was ready to talk with whoever set beside me but not looking for company. The last trip home being what it was, I was hoping I'd be wiser. And with so much having taken place the past few weeks, I took advantage of the ride to sleep. I got off the bus much as I had gotten on it two months prior, bearing a few scars but excited and filled with expectation.

I was excited to get home, as the last trip in I had found it to be a little difficult "pretending" that my folks and I hadn't just had a huge conflict, because my departure had caused a rift. This time, it was still a source of frustration and pain to them, but we were managing to talk. It was better.

I enjoyed a couple of nights at home and went to church Sunday and got my hug quota. That afternoon, however, I took off in the truck to meet up with Melissa and Pennie and catch up on life or at least as much as anyone was comfortable sharing. Before I headed home, I made one more stop by Gunny and Becky's but with new recruits on hands, I didn't hang around too long, and I just told them I'd be back the next afternoon. Becky hollered, saying their couch was still available so I should bring stuff to stay a couple of days. It's hard being in the military and not being by family. You give up family, and then when you get new orders, you give up friends. I was going to be leaving, but I was home now and we were friends. I'd be back tomorrow to assume my place on the couch, like old times.

Monday, Mom sent me into town to fuel up and wash the truck, and my brother and sister jumped in for the ride. It worked out well. *We* got to visit. The truck got a cleansing. We got McDonald's, and Mom got her stuff done. Besides, I needed to be dropped at Gunny's and Becky's, as I was spending the night there so it was all working out.

I was having a good visit with family and friends and was stoked about going to Japan when I reported back in January. To top that off, this time I got to fly to California to be shipped out, and I hadn't flown before. The sweetest part of all, however, was getting to spend the day with just Frankie and Angela. Without the folks around, we could just cut up and laugh like old times. Ah, it was good!

We had finished everything up and were coming down Race Street, passing by Harding and headed home, when my brother said, "Pull over. There's Lenny."

I didn't. I looked over and saw him waving at us and looked ahead, hoping to keep moving, but ughhhh, the light had turned. The cars in front of me were stopped. Crazy woman, I immediately saw him and came undone, not knowing whether I wanted to be angry, run, or … Here I was again. Come *on!*

My brother was calling me stupid and stuff. My kid sister started slapping the mess out of me (she might have been playing, but I don't think so and a tough black belt that breaks boards for fun; she hits hard). Sooo since I couldn't move forward I pulled in telling, them to do the talking, because I wasn't sure I had anything to say. He had been carrying in an armful of auto parts and was actually on the clock, so I wasn't surprised that we had to wait a minute.

But suddenly I was feeling super blessed because I thought I saw something. Yes! Yes! There it was again. It was snowing! Okay, just baby whiffs but my very *favorite* thing in the world was snow. Distracted, we started talking about what we were going to do if it snowed. Snowmen. Sledding. Eating snow cream!!! And then Lenny was at the door on MY side, and I was rolling down the window. I was really trying not to go back to where we had left off, but I kept wondering how much, if any, my hair had grown out since our last visit.

I avoided eye contact and Frankie faithfully kept up the conversation until Lenny asked me specifically, "Sherry, you want to go out tonight?"

My heart jumped, and that made me ... mad. (Yuppp, that's what emotion won out.) Well, I *wasn't* doing this stuff anymore. I had been too vulnerable with him LONG before I lost myself, and I wasn't going back there. It wasn't safe for me so I said, "No. I have plans tonight."

Frankie jumped back in talking, trying to divert what looked to be a train-wreck.

When Lenny tried to swing it back around I said we were going to be late and put the truck in gear and started backing off.

My siblings thought that was rude. That's me then—*just* rude. I'd been hearing it for a year now. Frankie told me all about it. And Angela repeated it once *again* and slapped the mess out of my arm. This time, I told her if she hit me again I was going to slap her back. Soooo there was *no more* hitting, but I did have to listen to them talk about what a great guy, he was and how he had been so nice, checking in on me while I was gone.

I couldn't get mad at them. I wasn't going to tell them what he was really like any more than I was going to tell them what I was really like. But they were right, and I had been rude. Just rude enough that I felt safe telling my sister she could call him and give him the Vance's phone number. If he still wanted to see me, he could call. That took the pressure off of me; besides, I didn't think she would look up his work number in the Yellow Pages. The kid I knew six months ago wouldn't have. This one did.

ℒ◦ℛ

I honestly didn't think he would call either but an hour later the phone rang. It was Lenny.

I said yes this time when he asked me out. Then I sat stunned and silent. Becky was the one person around when I had been drinking that weekend and I had told her ... *everything.* I had always wondered if she was sober enough to remember, but apparently, she remembered some of it. And she sat beside me asking me if I was okay, holding me as I was so still, except for the deep breaths I kept taking as I stared off into space. Concerned, she asked if she needed to call Vance. Shaking my head, I assured her I was going to be okay and forced a smile. Relieved, she shooed me off saying that if I had a date—which I guess I did—I should get ready.

I walked down the hall feeling like nothing was real, but the reality appeared to be that Lenny was going to be there around six. Closing the bathroom door, I turned to my reflection. I'd actually intentionally took off my civilian clothes as soon as I got to Gunny's, opting for my gold Marine Corps T-shirt and camouflage pants. I had on no makeup, because I rarely wore the stuff. My *still* too short, crazy hair was doing its own thing. I looked comfortable, ready to hang with the recruits and the Vances, *not* for a date.

That wasn't the problem, however. The problem was visible once again in my eyes. I could just think about him and my face got soft and pink, even now, and my eyes took on a light that made me know I was still way too vulnerable to do this. My brake had been dismantled, and that was all that ever kept me from giving myself away to him. The thought of him touching me filled me with fear. I wouldn't be able to say *no*. It wouldn't be a problem if it was anyone else, but I wasn't strong enough to be with Lenny. I slid into the floor, taking in what I was just admitting to myself as MY truth. I still loved him.

The only way I could see to get myself through this came in guarding myself. My heart. My flesh. I needed to get a backbone and an attitude. I wasn't going to spend the next three weeks, running after him or falling for his lines and getting shot in the heart. I didn't make the best decisions when I was down. I needed to think ahead and *jump* to what had become our *normal* ending first. Then maybe I could keep my guard up.

I sat there a long time going through our breakup. His return to the studio. His appearance at the skate rink. His appearance at my graduation. Let's not forget when I met him at the lake or before and after boot camp. Yuppppp that made it easy. I worked through the hurt and came into a calm fury and came out of the bathroom resolved.

A lot of attention had been focused on details for the evening but not on my clothes, hair, or makeup. He didn't know it, but this was going to be a "come as you are" date.

Mrs. Becky turned as I came up the hall. "That took you long enough. I thought—"

She stopped. "You didn't change … anything." She whispered as if it were a secret.

The guys had shown up and were eating, drinking, and playing poker, but she didn't have to whisper, because they weren't listening.

"No, ma'am," I replied. "I have dressed up for him before, and it didn't get me anywhere. And I'm not going out with him. We'll see if this runs him off, but if it doesn't and he asks me out to eat, he WON'T be taking me to McDonald's or Sonic. All those groceries I bought while we were dating they are going to cost him *if* he dares ask me out, because I want a steak and lobster, even though I won't eat seafood! He won't get my heart this time, Mrs. Becky, just the check."

It sounded so witty when I said it that I couldn't help but laugh. A confident laugh. I couldn't meet him with Jesus. Softness made me prey when I was with him. I didn't need to be wearing grace and mercy. I needed, *needed*, to be clothed in strength. Sadly, the quickest way for me to get there was to get mad and grab an attitude. And that is what I was doing.

Mrs. Becky didn't look so confident at all and merely shrugged and gave me the "I hope you know what you are doing" look before she went back to what she was doing.

He was there before I had time to evaluate my plan further. But as soon as I saw him—dressed up, looking great, smelling good, smiling at me—I knew I couldn't switch plans.

As I introduced him to the recruits, Gunny asked him if wanted something to drink.

Before I could say NO for him, he said, "Yes I'll take a screwdriver."

Oh, no he didn't! He just did NOT ask for a drink when he was with me!

Ohhhhh so that's how it was going down. NOW he *was* going to drink around me! I don't think so! Gunny hollered back to Bec to fix it, but I directed Lenny to the couch and told him, and them, I'd get it.

I was glad a wall was between us, as I had to ask Becky what a screwdriver was.

She actually started making it as she gave me instructions. "A little bit of vodka," and she poured it in, "and then you get the orange juice and fill it up. Tah-dah! A screwdriver."

I was hot. I was boiling M A D and mumbling to myself as I opened the fridge door. I didn't like drinking. I'd drank those couple of times, okay days not times, but I wasn't going to step back and date guys who did. People are stupid when they drink. I wasn't budging on that one.

When I turned back around with the orange juice, I asked, curious, "Why do you mix it with orange juice?"

"Because vodka is 99 proof and it burns and kicks butt, so you pull it down with the juice."

I remembered it burned and kicked butt, because I, in my insanity, had drunk mine straight *after* he, after *Lenny,* had got me all messed up. Shoot, I wasn't pulling anything down. I had started drinking because I couldn't cope with his repeated attacks on my heart.

I lifted the orange juice, as Becky watched, and added an inch of it to the inch of vodka that was already sitting in that twelve-ounce milk glass. Then I watched them merge to orange. Then I sat the carton down and grabbed the vodka bottle back up and filled it up!

Becky just shook her head as she put the orange juice in the fridge and I took off with "Lenny's screwdriver."

I smiled sweetly as I handed it to him, hoping he'd choke.

21

He may have swallowed a little quickly, but he took another sip as I sat down on the opposite end of the couch. He was in the middle of a conversation with someone at the poker table, so I just waited. His hair was too perfect. He was too pretty, really too easy on the eyes, I was thinking. Hmmm, I think maybe I have developed a strong preference for a more rugged look.

He was wearing a sweater that looked great on him BUT I preferred flannel.

He was sitting there still talking with one of the recruits, and if he talked much longer he wasn't going to have to walk out on me—hmm, I might just ask him to leave.

"Why are you smiling?" he asked.

"I was just thinking" was my response, which wasn't a lie.

Then came the questions about what I'd been doing and what he'd been doing, and I also asked how our mutual friends were doing, but it seemed he was spending as much time at the clubs in Little Rock as in Searcy since he'd turned twenty-one in August, so that conversation was short. One thing we didn't discuss was the past, or dating. That was intentional on my part, and most assuredly on his.

Then he asked me where I was headed next, and I told him Japan. He jokingly said he definitely wouldn't make it there. I not so jokingly said, "You didn't make it last time, either, so I'll be all right."

Then, to keep the frustration out of my voice, I told him about some of the training we had and the vehicles we had been able to drive (not everybody could say they had driven a Hummer in 1983, as they were still military transport not civilian back in the day), and a few of the people that were also going over with me. This included RJ, as regardless of our past, I was still the closest with him. I didn't mention anything about Eric or the stuff that had happened the last month or so. He did kind of hint around with questions, but I rolled them off.

Then he asked when I was taking off.

"Honestly, I don't remember. Sometime in January I report to San Diego."

"How long will you be gone?" It was question-and-answer time apparently.

But I was in. "A year."

"Why don't you just stay here?" WHAT!!!! Did he *really* just say that!

I almost laughed. "Because they would come and get me and I would go to the brig. That's why."

Then he said something selfish but honest. "Well … I don't want you to go, so how do you get out?"

I didn't even know what to think! A part of me wanted to get swept up because *he* was being vulnerable with a half-dozen men sitting 12 feet away. Another part, the part that had had a long conversation with herself in the bathroom just an hour or so before, that part wanted to tell him he had *some nerve* thinking I cared what he wanted.

But all I said was, "I'd *have* to be pregnant and I am not. SOoooo I am headed to Okinawa come January."

We sat with eyes locked—me on my side of the couch in my camis with my crazy hair and no perfume and him on his side looking perfect and polished and smelling good. Yet the longer I looked at him, the less resolved I became. He was searching too. I couldn't tell if he was trying to read me or if was wrestling with himself. I couldn't do this ...

It became more and more uncomfortable as the minutes passed, mainly because I could sense myself coming undone. I could feel everything trying to well up in me. A couple of times I had to check myself, because I felt tears rising up and my heart kept trying to resurrect something I couldn't chance. I breathed in deeply drawing my shoulders back and hoping to get my mind to override my heart. I was NOT going there again.

Not again. I would have moved but I couldn't.

My eyes were locked to his.

His to mine.

"Marry me."

He said it again, "Sherry, will you marry me?"

I think I quit breathing.

His eyes never left mine. I was studying his face trying to grasp what was happening even as he slid over and touched my hands.

I barely heard my answer, "Yes."

And he swept me into his arms and I was lost in what could only be a dream. Every impulse I had been fighting surrendered, and I melted. My heart's gates were flung wide open! I was vulnerable and delicate, yet I had never felt more alive.

When he pulled back, I felt radiant. And when I realized the guys playing poker were watching, my face flushed pink, but it turned red in the next instant, when Lenny turned to them and said, "Sherry has agreed to marry me. I'll have her back in an hour."

I didn't even ask questions as he led me outside and loaded me in his new truck. When he got in and had it running and the heater on, he pulled me back into his arms and took me to my favorite place. Then he said, "Let's go and let me ask your folks and make it official."

Off we went, 13 miles out of town, touching, talking, kissing, and then we were there. I didn't have keys with me, and so we actually had to knock on the door and wait to gain entrance. We could barely keep our hands off each other in the short time it took for someone to hear and get to the door.

Frankie was excited to see us and Angela grabbed Lenny's hand and practically drug him into the living room. Mom was just coming back in from their bedroom—dime on a dollar, she had already had her pajamas on when we got there and had to go change. Dad, well Dad hardly turned around to acknowledge us. He was in the middle of watching *Monday Night Football,* and he loved football. But also, where I was concerned, he had become a tad stoic.

Lenny wasted no time, not even waiting for a commercial or to have Dad's full attention.

Breathing deep, he just rushed in. "Herman, I have asked your daughter to marry me. If I have your permission?"

Dad turned around and looked at me, then Lenny, "Well, did she say yes?"

"Yes, sir," he said, tightening his grip on my hand.

Dad shrugged. "Good luck with that then. She tends to do what she wants." Not very edifying when you think about it, but my dad was not a very emotional man.

Luckily, Lenny had spent enough time with our family when we were dating that he wasn't even shocked or maybe he just had quit listening to Dad, as everybody else was ecstatic.

Eventually we ended back in Gunny's drive. And eventually we got out of the truck, and I leaned my back against his ride like old times. Then the weight of his body pressed into mine. There weren't any boundaries or brakes. It was amazing how different it felt to be held by SOME man and being held by THE man you loved. I was all in, not wanting it to stop. Now he was the one pulling back, as he also leaned back against the truck. Eventually our normal breathing resumed and we were both looking at the stars above. It was beautiful. Everything was beautiful.

Warm moments passed, but then I felt a chill in the wind, or maybe it was just in me as a nagging voice reminded me I wasn't the same girl anymore. I had to tell him. Searching for strength to speak, I knew I had to tell him I wasn't a virgin. I had a past. I came broken. I hesitated, afraid, but I wasn't going to start something I wanted to last our lifetimes with a lie. I had found it all and *once again* I was throwing out stuff heavy enough to sink us before we even got started. My eyes clouded over, or maybe that was the night, but when Lenny reached through the darkness and grabbed my hand, I started.

"Lenny?"

"Yeah?"

"I need to tell you something."

He stood upright, then searched my eyes in the darkness.

"I'm not a virgin anymore." I wasn't going to cry. If he needed to walk away, I'd rather him do it now. I waited as he leaned back again. He hadn't released my hand or quit caressing it, but it was so quiet.

I started praying. If he changed his mind again I was going to need to be stronger than ever before. I didn't have that kind of strength on standby. But never had I been so grateful to be redeemed and standing with the One who did.

When Lenny spoke, it was a question. "Were you when we were dating?"

I rushed in half shocked. "Yes, I was. But I had three weekends where I—"

He cut me off as he rolled over and pulled me to him, wiping the tears that brimmed my eyes. Looking into them, he said exactly what God had said that night just a week or so ago. "Doesn't matter. Sherry." His eyes compelled mine to lock on his. "It just doesn't matter."

He held me as I wept in relief and joy, and then we were doing what had always just felt so right for us. Man, I loved his kiss, his touch, the feel of him! I whispered under my breath. "If you want to make love now, I won't say no." He laughed quietly, looking at my face, my eyes, my lips. "No, ma'am, we waited this long we can wait a few more days." But his body implied something different and I was swept away. This was headier than any alcohol, which reminded me …

"Lenny …" might as well throw it all out there "I still don't like drinking or people drinking around me."

"That's probably good, because I don't like your screwdrivers."

We laughed. It was good to laugh.

He leaned back against the truck then and guided me over so that my back was rested against his chest. We both knew he had to go, but still we lingered in the silence, and I enjoyed his arms holding me like they'd never let me go and watching our breath rise in wisps of fog when we exhaled.

He laughed again and said, "You know that this is crazy. We haven't even been talking and have been broke up for almost a year. I *don't* even have a ring. I actually hadn't planned on asking you to marry me." It was gentle, sincere, honest and … overwhelmingly beautiful.

"That's fine, because if you'd have asked me when you walked in the door I'd have said *no*. I honestly didn't think my sister would call you and was prepared to dodge you the rest of the time I was home. But now ... now I'll tell you, 'I love you, Lenny Brewer,' and quite frankly it doesn't matter that I don't have a ring. It just doesn't matter." Then I rolled around facing him for one more kiss knowing I was going to have to go in because I was freezing in my T-shirt, and he was going to have to go home.

Leaning up from the side of the truck, he grabbed my hand and locked eyes with me again. I could have stood like that forever as we gazed in to the eyes and soul of the one whose heart made ours beat.

"I love you." He said it soft and low, and then he started walking me slowly toward the door. The quiet was almost magical.

But before I could open the door, he broke the silence once again with warm concern in his voice. "I know you don't care about a ring, but I'll bring you my class ring back tomorrow, as soon as I break up with my girlfriend."

Maybe someone else would have been upset, but I just smiled and leaned in for one more kiss and repeated, "It doesn't matter."

Conclusion

Darkness encompassed me thick and heavy. Noise, like broken chaos, was muffled in the dead of night. Yet in the whirl I sensed a hand at my back, sustaining me even as I fell. I was lifted, not washed away.

Where was the one, the one my soul loved. The one whose heart mine was chained to and I could not escape. The one that had forever been set apart as the holder of the keys to my heart. With eyes closed I searched, constantly fighting against the waves that threatened to pull me under.

Then the voice of the One that held me, spoke. So softly it came, softer than the whisper of a gentle wind. I couldn't hear it above the voices beside me. Pleading I asked, "What are You saying? Please ..."

And it came again. "Go to him. You have to go to him."

Before my mind could question where, the answer came, "Go back to where you left him. Hurry."

Breaking away from the crowd, I silently slipped through the night, weaving around the obstacles, vehicles, and forms around me. Then, finding solid ground beneath me feet, I began to run ... past the places where memories are stored and dreams are planted.

The tears flowed. As panic set back in gripping my heart ... was it even beating? I slowed, choking back the tears and gasping for breath so I could keep moving.

Then the voice came again. "You have to see him. Hurry before it's too late. You have to see him."

With all that was within me I raced toward what I could not see and wasn't sure I wanted to know.

But I ran hearing the voice behind me saying, "Hurry you have to see him again. Hurry ... hurry ..."

It remained echoing in my heart until slowly it started to fade. Then in fear the words were birthed on my lips, pouring over into the night watch. "I have to see him. Wait. Wait! I have to see him."

An urgency was born within me that gave wings to my encumbered heart. It bypassed the dreams. It bypassed the memories. It called for the tears and released the brokenness allowing room for nothing but this moment. As I ran into the night.

In the void I passed homes without light. Faces of strangers with questioning glances with no words. Faces I knew but that currently held no meaning … as my heart continued its push to my true love.

I ran toward the light at the edge of the darkness far ahead that beckoned me still repeating as I stumbled forward with the rasping cry of a lover calling out to the powers that be "Wait. I have to see him. Wait … "

It kept feeling like my heart had stopped. I clutched at my chest. Was it beating?

I finally arrived, so close I could feel him. My heart was undone. My eyes searched through the group that lingered near and in my way! They were in between me and Lenny.

"I have to see him. Where is he?" I had no other words, just a knowing that time was not my friend and these hands would help or hinder me from the one I must see, the one I would hold for eternity, the cheeks I would caress, the lips I must touch again with my own …

"Wait here," came an unknown voice from the darkness.

I stopped. I stopped the sobbing, caught my breath, and rose with a strength given by the Ones who walked in high places. I did not understand it. But I needed it and it was there.

He spoke again. "Follow me."

Two of my favorite words. Immediately they brought comfort to me as I recalled them from days gone by. Slowly I felt myself breaking free. I knew what lie ahead would lift me up above the storms that had held me captive all day even as it lay me down while I yet lived. But Lenny was before me. Every other beat of my heart was yoked to his. He was my pulse. The sharer of everything that had brought color to my life.

Evil whispered now from the shadows—no longer silenced they spoke of our great love. Of the injustice. Of his service. Of his grace and urged me to shout out and cry in anger and deny God's right to reign! I heard them and felt their weighty hands clutch at me. I could stop and succumb to the evil ... or move forward.

Faith urged me forward as my Lord silenced their whispers and heaven lifted my feet. Step by step to the side of a truck. Others stood there, but I had eyes only for one. And as he slid toward me, all the others faded away ... as beauty unfolded before me and the bag unzipped, revealing our new reality.

I took a final step closer 'til I stood at his side as the silent tears feel anew. I had seen that face in the moonlight so many times before. It wasn't so different from the nights we had spent leaning against his Camaro. Or in the back of his truck. Or laid upon a beach ... or lost in the presence of the One who had answered my prayer to "bring him back to me" so long ago.

My tears ceased as joy and peace flooded the depths of my heart to the furthest heights this soul could reach. And the nightmare ceased as I stood beside him, once again studying his face in the darkness searching his eyes for my completion. Drawing power from the light that gleamed there though we were shrouded in virtual darkness. I reached up to run my fingers through his forever flawless hair almost expecting to be reprimanded for messing it up.

"I love you, babe." An intimate laugh that was barely a whisper passed through my lungs as I continued gently smiling at him. "I know, I say it all the time. But I just never tire of saying it."

He remained unmoving beneath my hand as I ran one hand over his checks and rested the other on his chest. Then in the stillness his breath, like a mist on the water moved over me. It moved over my chest caressing my face with his words, "I love you too, babe." And I laid my head low to touch my lips to his own. For moments once again sharing, capturing the gift God had given to me. The touch of him. The taste of him. The feel of him.

Standing erect again, I let my eyes settle again upon his face. Still perfect. My heart smiled realizing his eyes were locked as well and still filled with passion.

Only two people had known the height and depth of that perfect light that lingered there now.

I was one.

I had seen it leaning against his truck on that December evening thirty-three years ago when he had asked for my hand and our hearts became forever forged. I had seen it as we fought battles, raised children, surrendered heart and home to a God who in His wisdom had yoked us to serve as one.

We had shared it in tears. We had shared it in triumph. We had shared it as we walked on the beach or sat in silence ... always just close enough to never be apart. We shared it as we lived our lives, ever heeding that still small voice that called us to go ... remain ... move ... pray.

We had experienced that fullness that was 'That Light' as we followed in faith together, soldiers with one mission.

We experienced it wrapped in each other's arms in the intimacy and honesty that two single-minded lovers find in each other.

It was a look born of honesty and intimacy that he reserved ... for God and me alone.

We three had walked through the valleys and been lofted on eagle's wings. Together we had experienced more life and love than most couples could find in a dozen lifetimes. Our hearts had pressed toward the prize eager to embark on the shores of eternity ... to know and be known apart from sin. It was the call we shared to any heart who would dare hear the message of a Risen Savior.

Our hope and expectation had long since been translated to a place beyond this world where we would stand perfected serving and walking side by side for all time.

The light still lingered in his eyes and, without words, revealed what would bring me strength for the hours and days ahead. He had seen Jesus. Redeemed he had risen from this world. He was and he was not because God had taken him by the hand and led him home ... leaving only what was necessary for my heart and those who remained to know.

I couldn't cry. I just gazed upon him in awe with all the love I had within me releasing into the stillness.

Leaning down, I spoke to him softly. "I know you've seen Jesus. I see Him in your eyes." Unheralded, a solitary tear fell from my cheek onto his own ... unbidden, it too had sprung forth eager to rest upon his skin. I reached over to wipe it away and by faith I heard the resounding ... of the only concern that would cause him pause as left that body.

It would be for me ... the one he cherished above all else. He had always covered me physically, even when he could not emotionally, financially or spiritually. Even in his weakness and in our struggles, his heart stood guard over my own, and my soul knew nothing sweeter than to cling to his. Even now he would ask God as he stepped away about my welfare. Imploring. Praying.

I heard the echo of it as I had bent in to wipe the tear from his cheek. Touching his lips once more with my own, I heard him and it stirred my heart with a love born from above. Thirty-three years of marriage, twenty-four years serving alongside each other in the ministry ... I could still feel his heart beat with need. And my voice in confidence rose up to reassure him as I gazed upon his face, "I'll be okay. As soon as I'm done ... I'll be right behind you, babe."

Then trailing my fingers one last time through his hair, along the tender lines that had come with age, lingering as they crossed his lips ... down, finally trailing to his bare chest ... I captured one more moment to freeze in time. Then looking to the men on his left and right I said with grace appointed for the hour, "Thank you." And I turned into the crowd of hearts God had assembled for such a time as this.

There are things in life that just don't matter.

There are times you will feel you, your dreams, your life is done. Those are the seasons to pray and surrender and wait on the Lord.

I share my journey and my shame, because *if* you can glimpse

God's sovereignty, His divine presence, through and in spite of my chaos, then *maybe* this journey can help you in your journey.

Maybe *you* won't run or be consumed when life brings in a storm. Maybe your heart will fall prostrate and embrace Him and the season and you will forge your way through firmly rooted without regrets. Or maybe you needed our story to be encouraged that today is simply a piece of your story but not the end. Maybe you needed to be reminded that *making* bad choices is different from *living* in them.

Battles are lost when fought on impulse, when based upon what our eyes can see. I gave away pieces of myself every time I wrestled against God's will. If I had been stopped short ... *No* ... if *he* had quit on us we would never have reaped the blessings we enjoyed on our incredible journey together.

God was faithful. God is faithful still.

You and I will struggle.

Yet the Word says the righteous will rise after each fall.

Don't kick someone when they are down. Look for the Jesus in every set of eyes you see and remember a lot of the things that seem so big ... *They don't really matter. They just don't matter.*

Apply grace liberally as some days you will be the rose on the vine, *but* on other days, you will be the thorn, and *then* you will need grace returned in equal measure.

Twenty-four years ago, today, Labor Day 1993, Lenny Brewer surrendered his right to live his life *his way* to the Lord. It saved our marriage, which had already weathered many storms, but at that time we were in the midst of one that threatened to wreck our vessel ... and annihilate our life together. When he surrendered that morning, the storm ceased.

In losing himself, Lenny became a champion, my knight riding in on a white horse to save the day. No longer vain or selfish, he was humble. No longer just seeing himself, he saw others. No longer "in love" with me, he truly loved me. And he was able to love others. The journey to that day is a whole other story I hope to share one day.

But while you are waiting, please do yourself a favor. Let go of what you think you hold so that you can grab hold of God,

the One who *knows what* you truly need

and who *sees* not only *who* you *are* but *all* you can be.

It's a journey you won't want to miss and a story only you can write.

Selah

Coming in January 2019

Their story continues with
That Man of Mine

CPSIA information can be obtained
at www.ICGtesting.com
Printed in the USA
LVOW10s0248150518

577104LV00001BA/19/P

9 781480 860995